SHOPPING for
CHRISTMAS

BY

PAT SIMMONS

This short story is a work of fiction. References to real events, organizations, or places are used in a fictional context. Any resemblances to actual persons, living or dead, are entirely coincidental. All Scriptures cited are from the King James Version Bible.

Praise for Pat Simmons

The fingerprints of books by esteemed Christian fiction author Pat Simmons are on file in the hearts of readers. *Every Day is Christmas* has the same identifiable features: commitment to Jesus Christ, Scriptures, romance, humor, close family ties, relatable trials and tribulations, and more.—Robin R. Pendleton

Waiting for Christmas. This book is amazing. I thoroughly enjoyed reading this book. Pat Simmons is the Queen of clean and Godly stories. I love it!!!! Ciara has a heart to give. Sterling and Ciara make a great couple, despite their own issues. It was awesome to see how their relationship blossomed into something beautiful. God, as always, is the reason for every season. Pat Simmons, may God bless your creative hand as always. —Rubykat

Christmas Takeover was a sweet family story that gives you a glimpse into how Christmas should be celebrated, Jamieson-style. Pat Simmons weaved a story filled with fun, humor, love, and change. Pace and Harmony will warm your heart with each look and conversation centered around the meaning of Christmas... Enjoyable, fast-paced read. —Msmagnolia Reads

Chapter 1

Imani Robinson was a hero. Like a mail carrier, she braved the elements through flash floods, dodging ice pellets, and lathering sunscreen to shield against the shooting sunrays. Yeah, Imani risked her life so that folks could eat.

She delivered food, including fish and chips for game night, medicine to the sick, and old-fashioned mama's recipes—such as soup, juice, and aspirin—for cold and flu symptoms. She even served as a nursemaid in a way, tending to babies' need for diapers, milk, and food.

To pay for grad school, she joined the ranks as a personal grocery shopper. Without a social life, shopping gave her human interaction. Customers ordered through the Home Delivery app. But, she would walk away from it all in two months with a Master of Public Health degree.

Now, it was time for Imani to give back—not the tips—but in another way to remind others that Jesus is the reason for the Christmas season.

Shuffling ideas in her head, Imani let her mind drift to one delivery, months earlier, which changed everything. It started with a familiar alert.

"You have reached your destination."

Imani remembered the story-and-a-half house's curb appeal. Three gabled dormers hinted that a bedroom occupied the upstairs. A plush green lawn resembled a golf course. Twin pots, with yellow and purple pansies stationed on both sides of the door, won her over. She sighed and patted her chest. Something about the color combination was whimsical.

From the sidewalk to the sage door, which blended seamlessly with the charcoal brick exterior, its charm beckoned outsiders to come inside for a peek.

She stopped gawking at the house to read the customer's instructions: *Drop off the order*, which meant she would leave the bags, take a photo to confirm delivery, then leave.

Imani weighed down her arms with as many plastic bags as she could carry and headed to Brandon J.'s porch for the drop-off. The door cracked open as if there was something sinister behind it. Then two excited children appeared, drooling for their goodies. They were adorable.

"Did you bring chocolate?" asked the younger child, a girl with warm brown skin that complemented her little brown doe eyes.

"Ah . . ." Imani mentally scanned the items ordered. It seemed like everything but that was on the list. "No, sweetie."

The little girl pouted and eyed the bags, strained with cookies, chips, frozen pizza, and juice. The latter, by the way, was getting heavy.

What parent allows their children to eat this stuff? Imani wondered. Didn't they know that childhood obesity increases the chances of developing type 2 diabetes?

A public health crisis.

Water, frozen vegetables, fresh lettuce with a few toppings, and chicken drumsticks seemed like an afterthought.

As Imani was about to hand each child a bag to relieve her load, another presence filled the gap. A perfect specimen of God's handiwork commanded the doorway. The tall, dark brown, muscular man distracted her. Too many words were scrambled in her head to describe him. Even his uncombed, thick black hair, which faded into his trimmed beard, was fashionable.

He eyed the bags, then the children. "What did you two order?" He lifted a silky black eyebrow and jammed his fist on his waist.

Sexy but intimidating.

"Everything," Imani mumbled as the children stood frozen, not answering.

Acknowledging her for the first time, his features softened. "Sorry. I left these two alone for five minutes, and this is the damage they caused. Need any help?"

"Brandon, right?" she asked, verifying that he was the customer. "Yes, please," then began to relieve her arms of the dead weight, which he passed to his children to take to the kitchen.

He stepped outside into the crisp spring weather in his house slippers, sweat shorts, and a long-sleeved T-shirt. Shivering for him, Imani pulled her thick, hooded cardigan tighter. She was cold-natured. But it was May, so the temperatures would start to warm up. He took the lead in walking to her car and shook his head at her trunk's contents. "This is all mine?"

The expression she gave him was his answer. Brandon seemed truly surprised by his children's activities.

Although this was two deliveries, the next customer's order, which was smaller, was in her backseat.

Brandon swiped the remaining bags and heaved the two water cases as if they were pillows. Imani blinked in disbelief as his muscles protested their entrapment.

"That was impressive. It would have taken me at least three more trips."

He shrugged off her compliment. "You'd think since they ordered all this food, they would be here to help."

Right! Imani kept that comment to herself. If she criticized his parenting skills, he might remove her tip from the order. She snapped a picture of Brandon and his groceries.

"Well, enjoy the rest of your day, and happy eating. If you're satisfied with my selections, I hope you'll give me a five-star review."

"You've earned ten stars." Brandon nodded and closed the door as Imani heard him yelling, "Aja, Tyler, don't think about opening any of this junk. . . ."

Imani snickered, but she hoped he wouldn't be too harsh with them. He was probably a great dad.

The house, the husband, and the kids. Some women had it all. If only Imani could order a practicing Christian for a husband online, she would put him in her shopping cart for delivery.

⸎

BRANDON JOHNSON MIGHT have been *briefly* distracted when he came to the door, but he didn't miss the shopper's understated beauty. His security camera had alerted him that a visitor was coming. The ridiculous number of bags reminded him of a trash dumpster or an unsupervised shopping spree, which I guessed it was. Home training prevented him from reprimanding the children in front of company.

He retraced his footsteps to his state-of-the-art kitchen, which offered a panoramic view of the great room, dining room, and deck. The builder's former display house was stocked with premium upgrades that enticed future homeowners to buy from this developer.

The decorator hadn't missed a detail, from the porcelain floor tile that complemented the front door's sage green color to the pearl-gray cabinets that blended with the white crown molding throughout the house.

Neighbors called it a wife's haven. Brandon didn't have a wife—yet—to share it with.

But back to his present crisis. Aja, five, and her brother, Tyler, who was seven, stopped ransacking the grocery bags that littered every available space on the L-shaped granite counters and stared up at him.

Crossing his arms, Brandon feigned a snarl. Six feet four inches tall and 230 pounds, mostly of solid muscle, would make others tremble. Those two? He couldn't intimidate them.

Aja and Tyler used their innocent expressions as weapons as they competed with him in a stare-off duel.

Brandon mustered a roar. "What did you two order while I took an important call? I said add one treat apiece to the shopping cart and hit send. That poor woman had to bring all that stuff to our door."

His niece and nephew, who'd been left in his care while their parents, Brandon's older brother and sister-in-law, were away at a conference.

"I know, but . . . we kept seeing pictures that said we could add to our cart." Aja's lips quivered, pleading their case.

Lifting his shoulders, Tyler bobbed his head. "Yep, that's what happened."

Brandon wasn't falling for it. "Who is supposed to eat all this stuff?" He pulled out party-size bags of chips and spied two six-packs of mini juices, in addition to the two cases of bottled water that Brandon had ordered, which the poor woman had to carry.

He paused his tirade. No, they didn't. Oreos? They were his favorite as a child, but wait. Brandon refused to be tempted as he rummaged through the bags for the drumsticks he'd planned to bake.

"We are, Uncle Bran." Aja gave him a dimpled smile like her mother's. She resembled a baby doll with her thick Afro puffs and chocolate skin. Aja had him and her daddy wrapped around her finger.

"But we're staying until the weekend, and we can't starve," Tyler tried to reason with him. His resemblance to Brandon was so strong that strangers mistook him for his son.

"Unless I put you two out."

Aja ran up to him and squeezed his waist in a bear hug. "But you love us."

"Mm-hmm." He hugged her back. "True, but I'm not falling for this. Your parents will have a fit if I let you eat this junk food. Pick out a couple of treats to keep, and the rest goes to a homeless shelter."

Aja shrieked in horror. "You can't give them junk food!" She threw his words back at him. "It's unhealthy."

The girl's theatrics didn't faze Brandon as he squinted. "Not working. I'm going to put the chicken and the rest of the food I ordered away, then we're going to look up a shelter or food pantry."

They groaned their disappointment as Aja stomped away, pouting and mumbling that he was unfair.

The joke was on Brandon. Never, ever shop online with those two again.

Now, what was Imani's story? The gold sweater she wore highlighted her fair, flawless skin. Unless her St. Louis Cardinals baseball red cap belonged to her father, brother, husband, or boyfriend, the woman was a baseball fan.

Brandon hadn't wanted to stare at the shopper, but he had to admire her beauty. He appreciated her sculpted features, including those cheeks and lips.

Yeah, he couldn't wait to place his next order.

Chapter 2

Most of Imani's customers faded from memory, but Brandon J. had resurrected her desire for companionship. Dinner for two at Tiffany's was only a fantasy without any prospects.

But something else nagged at her. Did the children's mother condone such bad eating habits? The family could benefit from an education on healthy eating rather than indulging in a food fest, although Brandon's physique suggested he hadn't formed an alliance with carbs.

After her next delivery, Imani signed off the app, achieving her monetary goal for the day. At home, she gobbled down her leftovers—stir-fried vegetables and cold crispy chicken. That left her an hour before her online biostatistics class started.

Studying was Imani's priority. She was fully invested in a career that would improve the health of communities. Imani had spent eight years as an archivist at the history museum until funding for the arts was cut.

Then she learned there was a skill to job hunting, and Imani didn't have it, so by default, she had filled in as a substitute teacher to share her love of history. But the income wasn't steady.

And that's when she'd stumbled upon the Home Delivery opportunity. Who knew there was a skill to eavesdropping in the dairy section?

"Yeah, man, if you need an extra couple hundred dollars a week, I can recruit you." There was a pause. "I make about a thousand a week and work my own hours and days."

Imani's jaw dropped. She was interested. By the time the two walked away, Imani had added six cartons of eggs to her basket when she had come for egg whites. She parked the cart and suddenly, just like that, Imani tuned into a stalker, trailing the red T-shirt guy from aisle to aisle. He moved swiftly and efficiently.

Yeah, they should talk. Imani retraced her steps to her cart, but it was missing.

"Oh, no." She stomped her foot. Some items had been the last ones on the shelves. Why did all shopping baskets look alike? Imani needed a kiddie cart with a flag.

Her mission was diverted again; she peeked into nearby baskets. Customers who caught her behavior gave her a warning, "don't even think about taking my stuff", or a "what's your problem?" glare.

That's what I get for ear hustling. Defeated, Imani gave up her hunt and decided to track down that red T-shirt guy for more information. He was at the register. As quickly as the clerk rang up the items, he bagged them as if he were their employee.

Imani looked at her target and headed toward the checkout, but her lost cart filled with her items came into view, parked near the pharmacy. She had to make a split-second decision: reclaim her groceries or leave them and chase after the man with the money. Imani gave up the hunt and finished her own shopping.

The next day, with limited information available, she searched online and signed up to become a Home Delivery shopper.

The man's boasting proved true. The tips were amazing. Week one, she earned an impressive amount despite getting orders mixed up and a missing tomato that rolled to the back of her trunk.

Week two, she was a pro, gliding down the aisles, following small flashing lights on shelves that alerted her to look "here" for the items. It was fun, but Imani didn't want a side hustle. She wanted a career, so she enrolled in school, and the grocery-shopping gig paid for it.

The classes were brutal. She had to memorize case studies, reading ten to twenty pages a day, taking quizzes, and attending weekly seminars via social media from professionals. Imani was mentally exhausted after the professor led a detailed discussion on the US public health research data from the last decade. She stood from behind her desk in her home office/spare bedroom, stretched, and sought refuge in her happy place.

An updated bathroom.

She soaked in the tub and pampered her skin with a luxurious vanilla-bean body scrub. Her mother's ringtone caused Imani to climb out, splashing water on the floor as she grabbed a towel to wrap around her. Imani ignored her wet footprints as she answered the phone in the bedroom.

Despite a thirty-year age difference, people often mistook the mother and daughter for sisters. Thirty-four and an only child, Imani was close to her widowed mother, Pauline Robinson.

"I haven't heard your voice today. You forgot to call and let me know you made it home from buying other people's food, as you insist on doing."

Imani stifled a yawn as she patted herself dry. "Sorry, Mom. After class, my body craved a hot bath, and you know how much I enjoy soaking. And the money is good for a couple of hours of work. Home Delivery is paying for my classes." If Imani recruited others, which she hadn't, she would earn bonuses. That would be even more money.

"Of course, if you had a husband, you wouldn't have to work so hard."

Sighing, Imani walked back into her bathroom and slipped as she reached for her body lotion. She landed on her bottom and dropped her phone, but quickly retrieved it. "Mom, I know some married couples who are struggling to get ahead. Plus, you've told me God is the greatest matchmaker."

"Yes, He is, sweetie. Get some rest. Talk to you tomorrow."

"Okay." Imani got on her knees, wiped the remaining water from her marble floor, discarded the towel, then climbed into her pajamas. She was about to say her nighttime prayers when her phone alerted her to a text Imani was tempted to ignore.

But curiosity got the best of her, so she peeked. Home Delivery had sent her a text: **Hi, shopper. Customer Brandon J. left a review and has increased your tip to $100.**

"What?" slowly escaped from Imani's lips. She blinked with disbelief. She enjoyed the gig because of the tips, but she had never, ever received one that big.

She read his review. *Imani was professional and friendly to my niece and nephew, even though they went overboard with the shopping. Ten stars if possible. Hope she will shop for me again.*

Not his children, huh? Why was that tidbit more interesting than the generous tip? She sent a generic thank-you, as direct communication between the shopper and the customer ended after delivery.

Interesting. Imani blushed and planned to keep lip gloss in her car in case she got another order from Brandon J. She wanted to be ready for their "next time."

BRANDON KEPT AN EYE on his niece and nephew after their stunt with the groceries yesterday. Their shenanigans would be the first topic of discussion when his brother called.

But that didn't happen. Kyle, Brandon's only sibling and two years his senior at thirty-eight, was always about business when he called, then moved on to Brandon's well-being, the house, or frivolous complaints. "How's everything going at the gyms?"

"We aren't reaching our clientele projection. If we could sign up more seniors, we would have steady revenue."

The brothers had used their inheritance money from their parents' deaths two years earlier to invest in a business of their own. Both men had had successful careers at Fortune 500 companies before leaving to open Time of Your Life, a joint venture.

With a targeted age group of fifty-plus, the brothers had two objectives: to keep clients motivated and active in their later years and increase their socialization. Their own parents hadn't exercised or maintained a healthy diet, and their lifestyles had triggered early disabilities. The gyms were the brothers' personal mission.

"Stop talking business, you two," Stacey said in the background. "What are my babies doing?"

"Honey, Aja and Tyler are no longer babies," Kyle said.

"Babies!" Brandon grunted. "Those two masterminds sabotaged my grocery order when I wasn't looking." He gave them a rundown of what the kids had done the day before.

Kyle's snicker crescendoed into a belly laugh. "Sorry, bro. You know I'm good for it."

"Or you're not. When was the last time you paid me back?" Brandon glanced out the window into his backyard, where the Johnson siblings were playing with Carlson, the next-door neighbor. "No need. I made them pack most of it and donate it to a shelter."

Stacey whooped. "You are so going to make a better father than your brother." She giggled.

"Maybe." He shrugged to himself. "Anyway, I plan to place another order tomorrow." Brandon rubbed his chin.

"Huh?" Kyle paused. "Why? Hopefully, you haven't overfed them. They beg for everything."

"Nope. Not about the food this time. It's the personal shopper who I hope will deliver it. You should have met her. If Imani has a man, he should be the one working extra, not his pretty lady."

"I thought you put a pause on dating until our businesses were thriving," Kyle said. "According to you, you didn't have time for the distraction."

"That was before Imani was at my front door." The woman might be out of sight, but she was definitely still on his mind. "Let me check the expiration dates on my milk and butter."

"Oh boy. This ought to be real interesting. We'll be home Sunday afternoon for Stacey's babies and see how this is going to work out."

Chapter 3

Imani wasn't thinking when she enrolled in the thirteen-month accelerated master's program, rather than the standard two-year degree.

The demanding homework didn't allow her to work for the same number of hours every week. Now that June was a few days away, the afternoons would be hot in St. Louis when she usually worked Home Delivery.

In a perfect world, if all customers gave bigger tips like Brandon J. had, she wouldn't have to play catch-up to meet her monetary goals.

"Lord, I need a blessing." She signed into her app, knowing she couldn't afford to be picky and turn down orders, while waiting for better-paying ones to come along. By the end of her shift, Imani had shopped for five customers. Brandon J. wasn't one of them.

On her way home, her best friend called. "Hey, Lynita. What's up?"

"Make any money?"

"A little. Not as much as I wanted." Imani didn't hide her disappointment.

"You can always enroll in nursing school, where the big bucks will be waiting for you after graduation."

Lynita's suggestion never enticed her. Blood, body fluids, and bed pans were about more than a big paycheck. Lynita had the compassion and stomach for it. "Ah, I'm good."

Lynita laughed. "Let's do something fun this weekend. I'm off."

"I'm not." Imani sighed. "This is my shut-in study weekend, so I'll be on lockdown."

After studying from early morning to until late afternoon, Imani signed into the shopper app the following week. The day was busy, and the tips were steady. One order caught her attention. Although it had forty-nine items, there was a generous tip, and the delivery was close to the store.

She snatched it before another shopper. With speed and accuracy, Imani finished, checked out, then packed the groceries in her trunk. She slid behind the wheel and read the delivery instructions.

Minutes later, her navigation said, "You have reached your destination."

Imani verified the GPS address of the modest white ranch home. She parked and activated her hazard lights, then began to remove bags from her trunk.

Although the front door was open, Imani still rang the doorbell. "Hello."

"Bring the groceries inside! I'm disabled," Ralph W. yelled.

Opening the storm door, Imani was startled to see not one but two older White gentlemen who might have weighed about three hundred-plus pounds each, more than double her weight. Creepy. Somehow, the furniture supported them.

"Ralph?" she asked, looking from one man to the other, wondering if both were disabled.

"That's me," he said from his perch on the sofa, raising his hand.

"Do you mind putting those in the kitchen around the corner? Sorry. I have neuropathy."

"Sure." Imani did as Ralph asked, noting the small, outdated, bright yellow kitchen walls. Not a disaster, but untidy.

The unidentified man, who squeezed into an oversized dark paisley chair, said nothing as he tracked her movements. He made Imani uneasy with his beady eyes, putting her on guard.

She returned to her car for the remaining plastic bags and loaded them into her arms. She didn't care how heavy. A third trip inside wasn't happening.

Imani followed the trail to the kitchen, praying someone wouldn't jump out of the closet or another hiding place. Task done, she made a beeline for the front door. "That's it."

Ralph asked, "Are you a Christian?"

Huh? Imani didn't want to press pause as she whipped her head around. *Lord help me, because this was not the time for an evangelizing moment.* "I am."

Ralph's smile didn't reach his eyes. "Have a seat. Where do you attend?"

"Holy Ghost Temple." Imani glanced at her phone. "Sorry, I'm on a schedule and can't stay."

"Oh." Ralph sounded disappointed.

She rushed out the door as if she was being chased, jumped into the car, and locked the doors. Her heart pounded louder than a barking dog. Imani confirmed the delivery and exhaled.

The devil appears as an angel of light. Do not go inside another house! God's voice thundered.

The Lord didn't have to tell her twice. What danger hadn't He shown her?

Shaken, Imani backed out of the driveway. Her phone alerted her to a new order. How could she accept it when she was recalibrating from the eerie feeling from inside that house? Plus, she replayed what God had said.

At a stoplight, Imani was alerted to another order. She glanced at her phone with no intention of taking whatever it was.

Against better judgment, Imani accepted the order. It was for Brandon J.

She had regulated her breathing, but her hands shook as she gripped the steering wheel. Brandon had requested Dierbergs, an upscale grocer. At the store, Imani did her best to clear her head as she shopped for a Gatorade variety pack, fruits, beef, and pasta. Different choices from the last time.

A smile tugged on her lips. Brandon was health-conscious. She checked out and packed the trunk.

Twelve minutes later, her navigation announced, "You have reached your destination."

Her spirit settled as she parked in the driveway and activated the hazard lights. Brandon stood in the doorway, leaning against the frame with his arms folded, and grinning.

Glad someone was having an uneventful day, Imani popped the trunk. While gathering the bags, Brandon appeared beside her. Spooked, she jumped, and her heart raced again.

"Are you okay?" Brandon's frown showed his concern.

She coaxed herself to calm down before she answered, "Yeah."

"Finally, my favorite personal shopper has showed up."

His compliment distracted her. Imani studied his face and noticed that the sunlight revealed glimpses of the brown hues in his eyes. He heaved the bags of groceries with one swoop, leaving her with nothing to carry.

"Show-off." Imani chuckled as her old self resurfaced.

"This was my fourth order this week, hoping to get you again," he said matter-of-factly.

Fourth? She blushed. "Really?"

His admission seemed to make everything all right in her world. After confirming his delivery, Imani signed off the app. "Last order for me." She might as well end the day on a flattering note.

PERFECT. Brandon was not about to let Imani escape so easily.

She was as beautiful today as she had been the first time he saw her, which seemed so long ago. Despite the heat, she wore the same red cap.

Brandon was tempted to remove it to get a full view, but he did notice the pink lip gloss. He conducted a quick assessment: five-seven, tops, about 135 pounds or less, and single.

The finger check was a common practice whenever a man saw a beautiful woman. If a diamond claimed the fourth finger, Brandon backed off.

A cool breeze teased her hair trapped under the cap.

"I was surprised by your small order today," she joked.

"Right. I donated most of the first order to a shelter. I treated my staff to the recent orders. Wait, let me put this on the porch."

Her phone chimed.

"You have to go?" He panicked, not hiding his disappointment.

"I thought I had signed off." She sighed. "You're my last order. Trust me."

Brandon exhaled, jogged to the porch, and released his load. *Yes!* "Since you know where I live, you're welcome to stop by and visit."

Fear flashed in her eyes. "Why would I do that? I don't know you."

Did she feel threatened? Maybe Brandon was invading her space. He stepped back. "We can exchange numbers and get to know each other."

"You can connect with me on social media." Imani reached for her car handle.

He twisted his lips, not happy about her option. "So you can block me at any time?"

"I won't, if you aren't a stalker." Her voice was shaky.

"Never been accused of that one." Brandon pulled out his phone and tapped one of the social media icons. "Imani . . . ?"

"Robinson."

Brandon scrolled through several with the same name, then stopped when he recognized her. He grinned as he studied her profile pic. "Gorgeous smile. I just followed you. Follow me back . . . please." Brandon opened her car door. "Be safe."

"Thanks. I will."

Behind the wheel, Imani began backing up, then jammed on the brakes. "Wait. Do you have a wife, past wife, future wife, current lady, or children?"

He did his best not to smirk. *So she was interested.* "None of the above."

"Okay, then we can be friends on social media." Imani waved and drove off.

Brandon slipped his hands into his pants pockets and watched her taillights disappear down the street. Imani Robinson had no idea that he wanted to be more than friends.

Chapter 4

Imani was impressed when she checked Brandon's social media profile. Or maybe not. Brandon had thousands of women friends. Should she be jealous that she was now on his roster? To his credit, most of his photos were either inside a gym or with family.

Brandon resembled his brother. Hmmm. She forced herself to stop looking. He had asked to be friends, and they were.

Enough. She didn't have time for distraction while in grad school.

In the days that followed, Brandon sent her private messages. She was slow to answer and when she did, her responses were brief.

For weeks, Imani never saw another order from Brandon J. She tried not to give it much thought. Then it happened when Imani grabbed two orders, one of which was from him, and both deliveries were close together.

Would it be odd for Imani to see Brandon again? "Doesn't matter," she coaxed herself, shaking herself free of worry. Imani had one goal: earn a hefty paycheck, mostly of tips. She completed shopping, checked out, and loaded her trunk with the customers' orders.

She was both relieved and disappointed that Brandon wasn't standing in the doorway like he had the last time. His instructions were to meet the customer, so she had to face him. Arms overloaded with his groceries, she managed to ring the doorbell. Just then, a gray sports car barreled down the street, screeched to a halt beside her car, and Brandon jumped out. "Sorry. Problem at the gym."

"Excuse me?" She frowned and admired his physique. Imani tried to avoid ogling him as he relieved her of the load. A breeze stirred his cologne and tickled her nose. She groaned inwardly.

"My brother and I own two fitness centers," he explained. "It's on my profile page."

She hadn't perused it. That explained the gym photos. *How can he smell so fresh?* "I could have left it on the porch and taken a picture to confirm delivery."

Brandon rested his hands on his waist. "And miss the opportunity to see you and ask for your number?" He shook his head.

He had already asked for it via private messaging. Now, that they were face-to-face, Imani wasn't sure what to do, so she changed the subject. "Ah, I commend you for stepping out by faith and opening a business. That's impressive."

"Not if I don't trust God to bring about an increase. Businesses can never have enough patrons. Signing up more seniors will help *Time of Your Life* locations thrive. We have a welcoming environment and offer age-appropriate exercises to keep them active."

Intelligent, ambitious, plus he was handsome. Imani needed to rethink her opinion of him.

Since Brandon seemed locked on his spiel, she didn't dare interrupt him. "The demographics are there. It's getting the word out to our target audiences—churches and senior residence homes—to discuss exercises to improve mobility, balance, and mental health. Plus, the government pays their membership fees if they are enrolled in Medicare's Silver Sneakers program."

Imani studied him. "I apologize for misjudging you the day I delivered all that unhealthy. . ."

"You can go ahead and say the word—junk food." He laughed.

"True." Embarrassed that he had read her thoughts, she looked away briefly. "I never realized how our policies affect our health. I want vulnerable communities to overcome the odds, so I decided to return to school and earn my master's degree. I pray I can make a difference."

Now, she was giving him her spiel. Surprisingly, Brandon was easy to talk to. Imani was about to share something else when her phone alerted her to available orders. She accepted one that would help exceed her daily quota.

As she turned to leave, Brandon stopped her. "Before you go, may I ask why you're delivering groceries?"

"The money. The tips cover most of the cost of grad school. I enrolled in a thirteen-month program, so come December, not only will I celebrate Christmas but my second degree."

Brandon seemed thoughtful. Something was on his mind. "May I?" He reached for her hand, catching her off guard.

"Father, in the name of Jesus, please bless Imani's endeavors, protect her from harm, and dangers seen and unseen," he paused, "and let her receive big tips. . . . And give her happiness."

Breathless, Imani was stunned by his sincerity and concern. Overcome with emotions, she inhaled and exhaled. "Thank you."

A man who prays, stays. Her mother's words seeped into her mind.

Imani couldn't let this be one-sided. Brandon had prayed for her, so she wanted to do something for him. "Look, I'll ask my mom to talk to the seniors at our church about visiting your gym."

His eyes widened in hope. "Thanks, and the invitation is open to you too. And so is a dinner invitation—not at my place, but a restaurant of your choice."

"You're making it hard for me to say no."

"Then don't." He stepped closer. "I still would like to have your number."

She gave his request one last consideration before giving her answer. "Okay. As for dinner, how about a raincheck? I have to focus on school." *And spending time with you would be a distraction.*

"Four months." Brandon groaned, then bobbed his head. "As long as we can talk."

That was still a distraction, but they exchanged numbers. The excitement on his face matched that of his niece and nephew when they had greeted her at the door.

Imani hid her excitement. Brandon had prayed for her happiness, and right now, she was happy, looking forward to that dinner date that was a season away. But he agreed to it.

"I'd better go shopping."

Brandon held the door open for Imani to get into her car. As she backed out of his driveway, he watched, then suddenly, he stopped her.

"Oh, one more thing. I like your lip gloss!" He lifted a brow in a flirt, then turned and headed to his house.

Imani blushed. He had noticed.

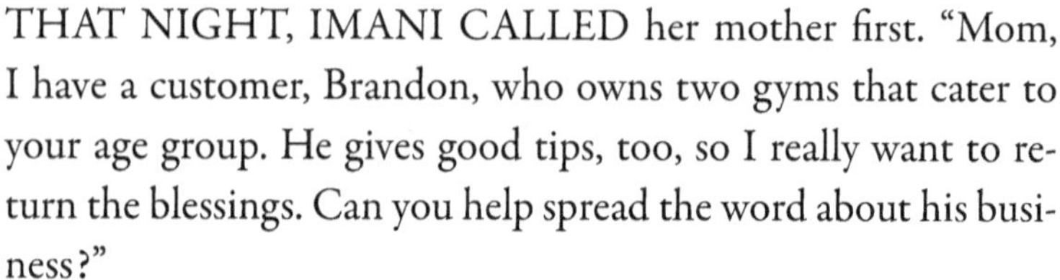

THAT NIGHT, IMANI CALLED her mother first. "Mom, I have a customer, Brandon, who owns two gyms that cater to your age group. He gives good tips, too, so I really want to return the blessings. Can you help spread the word about his business?"

"Is he married?" The mischief played in Pauline's voice.

"No."

"How does he look?" The interrogation continued.

"What does that matter?" Imani feigned annoyance while containing a grin as her mother pressed for a description. "You would probably call him suave, and he prayed for me."

"*Humph. Humph. Humph.* A man who prays, stays," her mother said as if she was savoring a mouthful of collard greens. "I guess I'd better help. Brandon could end up as my future son-in-law. I'm on it. Night, baby."

Chapter 5

Imani had mixed emotions when Brandon didn't call her the same night. She got over it and concentrated on what was important—her studies.

A few days later, she received a text from him: **At the gym. Thinking about you. I won't call and disturb you. Shopping today?**

So she *had been* on his mind. **Yes. I'm starting later than usual this afternoon. I have a lot of reading so I can pass these self-guided quizzes.**

With zeal and focus, Imani examined the health disparities in non-White populations. The rates of chronic disease, infant mortality, and women's health complaints were disturbing. But if she was going to work in public health and policy, Imani had to come before businesses and lawmakers armed with proof and suggestions on how to do better.

She memorized the stats broken down into age brackets for different racial and ethnic groups, such as Black, American Indian/Alaska Native, and some Pacific Islanders.

When Imani completed the last of three quizzes, she shut down her computer, stretched, and dressed comfortably. Time to get to work.

A big order seemed to be waiting for Imani when she signed into her Home Delivery app. She snagged it and shook her head in disbelief. Brandon's timing was impeccable.

Imani called him. "Really? You need groceries?"

"Guilty." She could hear the smile in his deep voice. "I'm still at the gym, but I plan to head home to receive my groceries from a very beautiful shopper who has to meet the customer. I'm making soup. Too bad it won't be ready for you to take it to go."

Thoughtful. "Thank you for offering. See you soon," Imani said softly and ended the call.

At the store, Imani had two orders. She smiled as she picked up Brandon's vegetables and stew beef. His seasonings—celery seeds and rosemary—made her mouth water. Mike W.'s order was a contrast: pizza, chips, cookies, soda—a lot of liters—deli meat and dip. She finished shopping in her allotted time, then Brandon added an item with a note. *Red roses. For you.*

Imani's breath caught.

Her eyes teared.

She swallowed hard.

Sweet. Brandon's thoughtfulness made her heart flutter, doing somersaults to the landing. Flowers before they had a date. This small gesture was powerful.

In the car, Imani called Lynita. When her friend answered the phone, Imani started, "I got roses. Brandon ordered them while I was shopping and told me to pick them out myself and . . ." She rambled out as much information as she could while following the navigation to her first delivery.

Lynita fussed when Imani told her that she had put dinner on hold with Brandon.

"Girl, you can have it all. A better career and a new man. I love it!" Lynita screamed.

"I wish." Imani grunted. "Do you know how many hours I have to study, attend webinars, and interview professionals?"

"So?" Lynita *tsk*ed. "Getting a BS in nursing isn't soft like cream pie either, but I dated."

"And broke up at least two times, but anyway, don't forget some shopping shifts are longer, depending on whether I meet my daily money goal early, or not. Where is there room in the middle of my life between work and school? I have to sleep."

Nothing Imani had said convinced her friend to side with her. The new development made Lynita push harder.

"I'm almost at his house. Got to go." To her delight, Brandon was there and strolled to her car. Admiring his physique, she noted a slight bow in his swagger. The man was fine.

"Whew. I beat you by three minutes." He grinned triumphantly and opened her car door. "You're spoiling your shopper." She showed him the red roses and sniffed. "Thank you."

Brandon eyed them, but his gaze lingered on her and her lips. "Good choice."

She didn't have her lip gloss on. Was he looking for it?

He helped her step out after she popped the trunk. As Brandon reached for the bags, Imani stopped him. "Wait. These are two separate orders. I don't want you to get them mixed up."

"Okay." He moved back, waited for her instructions, then he took the bags. Imani swiped to confirm the delivery and groaned at the location of the next order.

"What's wrong?" Brandon frowned.

Gritting her teeth, Imani slowly exhaled. "My next delivery is about eight miles away, and that zip code isn't in the best neighborhood."

"Hold on. Let me get my keys, and I'll follow behind you." With plastic bags in tow, Brandon jogged inside and returned with his keys as she protested.

"I have pepper spray," Imani objected, trying to sound brave. After all, this was her livelihood.

Let him go with you, God whispered.

"I insist." Brandon stepped closer.

"Thank you."

Brandon activated his garage door, and a black SUV was parked next to his sports car. His vehicle had dark-tinted glass, as if he were part of a Secret Service detail.

Shopping later meant delivering at night. Imani thought about Ralph, and that had been in daylight. It had taken her a while to get over that uneasiness, and God hadn't given her a heads-up. Now, the Lord had.

Imani followed the navigation path for about ten minutes with Brandon trailing behind. She turned onto a street where shadows overpowered the few lights that served as beacons of hope in the neighborhood.

Brandon called and she answered through her Bluetooth. "You see that lady cutting tree branches in the dark?"

"Yeah. I don't know how she can see or why she's doing that." Suspicious activity came to mind.

"Seems like a setup to me."

Perhaps. Imani prayed Brandon was wrong.

Chapter 6

What happened to leaving a porch light on for ya? Brandon wondered, paraphrasing an old Motel 6 commercial.

He watched as Imani turned her car into the driveway of a house that could be vacant—or worse, a crime scene. "Please don't let this woman—a dinner date away from possibly being my woman—get out. Please, God." On high alert, Brandon was ready to defend.

Brandon glanced around. The lady across the street never stopped trimming her tree. "You won't win a 'nosy neighbor' award."

Imani activated her hazard lights and honked her horn. A man emerged from inside the house. He blended with the darkness of the night, and the blackness of his house, and the shadows of the neighborhood. *Do they not have electricity, or is this a setup for an unsuspecting and beautiful shopper?* Something was off.

"I'm Home Delivery with your groceries," Brandon heard Imani say from the trunk of her car.

"Yeah, yeah. You need help?" the man asked and looked over his shoulder into the dark house.

Hands reached out from inside. *Yeah, Imani should not be here alone.* Brandon exited his vehicle and trekked swiftly to her side. "I got this," He said behind Imani as he heaved six cases of soda.

Imani's eyes said it all.

Gratitude.

Showing no fear, Brandon approached the man and not too gently shoved the soda cases into his waiting arms. The customer grunted.

Imani waved. "Thanks for using our service. Night."

Brandon returned to her side, still on guard for possible threats and ready to respond. In a calm voice, he asked, "Is this your last order?"

"Yes." She nodded with a spooked expression.

"Let's go." He waited for Imani to get in her car and lock the doors.

Back in his SUV, he called Imani through the Bluetooth. "Do you know how to get out of this neighborhood?"

"I always program the GPS to take me back to the store."

"Okay, babe." Did he just say that? The endearment slipped. But Brandon had no regrets. After tonight, he was fully invested in Imani, whether they were in an official relationship or not. "Can you pick a public place so you can decompress?"

Not a fan of talking while driving, hands-free or not, Brandon's mind shouted for him to stay connected. Soon they arrived at a twenty-four-hour sandwich shack. He parked next to her, stepped out, and rounded the bumper to open her car door.

Permission not asked, but Brandon hugged Imani as she collapsed into his arms, shaking. When she did pull out of his embrace, he searched her eyes for fear.

Gone.

Instead, he saw peace. Good.

"Ready to go inside?" Although the night had cooled after the sun had set, Brandon would stay outside all night or in their vehicles, if that was what she wanted.

"Yes."

Taking the liberty, Brandon linked his fingers through her trembling ones.

Imani didn't protest, so they walked inside hand in hand.

Your Pleasure Food was a small restaurant. The lights were dimmed over dozens of tables, creating a relaxed atmosphere. The olive-green interior complemented the almond-painted shutters. Patrons were sprinkled throughout the place.

A young male clerk with long, neat locs greeted them at the counter.

The pair perused the menu, which boasted burgers and fries in the evening, pastries and bagels in the morning, and not much else in between.

"Anything look tempting?" He glanced at her. Her baseball cap, which he was accustomed to seeing, was gone, and the weariness on her face made him want to hug her forever.

Restraint was not his mentor when he yearned for the freedom to explore a relationship.

"I'm not really hungry." Imani shook her head for emphasis.

"You might be once your adrenaline returns to normal. Take it home for later," he pressed and patted his chest. "For me, please."

She smiled and her eyes brightened, erasing the tension. "Okay. How about a turkey burger with Swiss cheese?"

Brandon ordered the same and added a lemonade.

"Is this for here or to go?" the clerk asked.

"Here," they answered in unison, sharing a smile.

Imani chose a booth for two near a window. He sat, facing her. While they waited for their food, Brandon stared, not only to admire her beauty but to gauge her mood. "What happened back there was weird. Is this what you go through all the time?"

Brandon's imagination stirred up deadly scenarios.

"I try to be safe, even in the daytime. I have my pepper spray, but I felt uneasy. The house and street were shrouded in darkness, and people were outside doing odd things in the dark. I saw one guy looking under the hood of a car." She shivered. "When you offered to go, I heard the Lord speak to let you, and I appreciate you."

"Really?" He nodded. "That's interesting, because when I least expected, God told me to pray for you. After what I saw and felt tonight, I see why."

The server appeared with their food. Brandon reached for her hands again. "Lord, thank You for protecting Imani from dangers unseen tonight and every day she shops. Thank You for allowing us to cross paths. And bless our food and the hands that prepare it, and remove all impurities. Help us do our part in feeding those who are hungry. In Jesus' name. Amen."

Imani relaxed and smiled. "I like the sincerity in your prayers."

Her compliment made him blush, then he recovered. "What did you do before becoming a personal shopper?"

"Most recently, I was a substitute teacher after my position was eliminated at the history museum. I loved my job as an archivist." Disappointment touched her face as she took one bite, then another. Her appetite had returned without her realizing it. "As a sub, I quickly learned in education that some parents were the problem that caused the children to become problems."

Face-to-face, Brandon had a chance to study her facial expressions: regret over losing her job, yearning for her late father, and happiness that reached her eyes when she spoke about her upcoming graduation.

"Once I graduate, I'll officially end my status as a shopper." She giggled. "I might never go inside a store again to shop for myself and instead use their service."

Brandon chuckled with her. Her eyes drifted as she glanced around the restaurant. What was she thinking?

Resting her elbows on the table, she leaned forward. "Before hanging it up, I would like to give back to my favorite customers."

"What do you have in mind? I'll be an accomplice." He wiggled a brow.

When she yawned without revealing her plan, Brandon called it a night. "Mind if I pray for you now?"

"Please do."

He loved the feel of her hands as he gathered them. "Father God, in the name of Jesus, protect Imani's going out and coming in. Please supply her financial needs to finish school so she won't be in danger. Thank You in advance. In Jesus' name. Amen."

"Amen." Imani sniffed and stood.

Brandon began to collect their discarded trash. "The next time you have to deliver late, please let me go with you."

As she tilted her face toward his, Imani's lips curled into a smile. "What woman can resist a handsome bodyguard?"

"I hope not you." Squeezing her hand, Brandon led her to the door.

Chapter 7

Imani was convinced that Brandon was God's gift to women. His features were created with care. It seemed as if the Lord had placed one black lash at a time on his lids. His jawbones and silky mustache made him stand out. He was a protector—it had nothing to do with his height, bulk, or grip that showed his strength, but the prayer warrior within him. With all his assets, he possessed a generous supply of calmness in a volatile environment.

Then there was Brandon's hug—so comforting.

She walked through her door, giving praise and thanksgiving to God, then called Lynita. "You'll never guess what happened to me tonight."

"Hmm, you didn't get robbed or carjacked, because you sound too happy."

"Girl, please. No carjacking or robbery. That's probably what the devil planned, or worse, because I try to avoid any deliveries to the Cassville area, but I had to go there tonight. I'd just delivered to Brandon, and he must have sensed my apprehension and offered to trail me."

"A man who steps up without you asking!" Lynita didn't contain her excitement and snapped her fingers in the background. "I love it. What else? There has to be more."

Imani grinned. "There is." She relayed what happened. "Then I fell into Brandon's arms outside the food place."

"Of course you did."

"The funny thing is, it didn't feel awkward. I like him," Imani said, pacing her bedroom floor, "and his prayers for me seem sincere. He called me babe as if it was the norm."

His endearment and willingness to drop whatever he had planned to ensure her safety made Brandon a winner.

While chatting about the pros and cons of her dating while in grad school, Imani received a text. **Home?**

"Lynita, I've got to go. Brandon just texted me, asking if I had made it home." Imani ended the call and texted him back. **Yes. Thank you for being there tonight.**

She was tempted to call him, wanting to hear his rich voice or imagine his eyes twinkling when he laughed or his frown when he was concerned. "Wow."

Imani prepared a hot bath, then remembered she hadn't called her mother.

Pauline's sweet voice greeted her. "Praise the Lord for protecting my baby on those streets."

You have no idea. "Amen. Brandon trailed me to my last delivery." She left out the reason why. "Afterward, we had turkey burgers."

"I like him! I feel better knowing God sent him."

Imani frowned. "Why do you say God sent him?"

"When a mother prays, God lets us know things about our children, and I've been praying for your safety. Hallelujah! Good night, dear."

Shaking her head, Imani sniffed. "Lord, thank You for prayer warriors."

As she knelt to say her nighttime prayers, eager to climb into bed and allow the night to fade into a distant memory, Imani felt God's presence nudging her to continue.

Pray for Brandon as he has prayed for you, God whispered.

"Lord, I know he wants more memberships for his gyms. You know what else he needs and wants. Bless Brandon in ways unimaginable in Jesus' name. Amen."

"MAN, THAT'S A ROUGH way for her to earn money to pay for grad school," Kyle said on the phone when Brandon told him about what had happened.

"Yeah. I can't believe she has to deal with that," Brandon said as he peeked out of his bedroom window into the night sky, glad that Imani was safe at home.

Brandon admired the pond, not far from his house, which cradled the moon's reflection. He wished Imani were with him to appreciate the night sky.

"Hey," Kyle said, putting a halt to his wandering thoughts, "why don't you add her on the payroll?"

Twisting his lips, Brandon shook his head. "I'm into her, and I don't mind helping as I get to know her, but that's extreme. Plus, I think she's more independent than a damsel in distress. She may look at it as charity."

Kyle grunted. "Yet she accepts gratuity. The irony of that."

Brandon rubbed the back of his neck, frustrated that he couldn't solve Imani's problem. "I don't like that she compromises her safety for tips. Anyway, our payroll is tight until the advertising pays for itself in new members."

"You'll think of something. Wait. Aja and Tyler want to talk to their favorite uncle."

Brandon laughed. "Okay. I'll talk to my favorite niece and nephew," was his comeback.

Aja wanted to ride her bike to his house, which was at least ten miles away.

"No. I live too far," Brandon told her. "I'll come and get you soon."

Tyler took the phone. "Uncle Bran, don't forget to come to my first soccer game."

"Got it on my calendar, buddy." Brandon couldn't wait to have his own family so Kyle could become a favorite uncle.

The call ended, and Imani's soft features invaded his thoughts. Brandon had no right to have an opinion, but it was dangerous to go to strangers' houses—period. Forming a plan, he opened his laptop, signed into the subdivision's website, and composed a blog post:

Hello Fellow Neighbors,

If you use Home Delivery for groceries, like me, please tip—the more, the better. Although the company is gouging us with high delivery and service fees, I learned from one shopper that most make between seven and nine bucks per order, which could include two or three customers. And the average shopper could work up to nine orders per shift.

Brandon paused, considering whether he could make it personal, because at the moment, it was about Imani.

One shopper told me she has to accept five orders, sometimes more per shift, to make money to pay for grad school. Basically, it's our tips that cover her tuition, not what Home Delivery pays.

We have a great neighborhood, so I'm asking us to be generous. Brandon Johnson, 3756 River Bluff Court

A few replies came within seconds.

I live around the corner. Thanks for letting us in on the inside scoop. Will do. Craig.

Hey, neighbor. I'm three doors down. I've always wondered what these shoppers' stories are. Thanks for the enlightenment. Will do. David.

More favorable responses popped up. Brandon was proud of his neighborhood. What more could he do to help Imani?

Pray, and I'll open the windows of heaven and pour out a blessing she won't have room to receive.

Imani needed that Malachi 3:10 blessing. So did Brandon. The best way for him to be blessed was to put others' needs before his own. "Lord, let it rain tips . . . and sane, safe customers. In Jesus' name. Amen."

Chapter 8

Good morning. This is Imani. About last night: I appreciate you for being there and praying for me. What can I pray for you? She sent the text early the next day, before taking a series of practice quizzes.

Brandon responded immediately. She hadn't expected him to be up early.

I'm glad you allowed me to go. I don't want anything to happen to my pretty personal shopper. :) I solicit all the prayers from anyone, especially ones for our gyms to thrive.

Right. Her mother was on that because she loved any mission. And Mama would come through. It might not be right away, but it would happen, "according to God's will," she always said. If Brandon's business was struggling, his hundred-dollar tip and the generous ones after that were sacrifices.

Where are your gyms?

In a romance playbook, Imani would take him lunch. If only she had time to pivot from her schedule. Of course, Lynita was cheering her on with "Get the money, education, and the man."

Imani *hmph*ed. They weren't in an official relationship. Yet her heart whispered something different. Brandon had been there for her. **What's your address?**

He texted back two locations: North City and North St. Louis County, but he was at the one in the city today. With that tidbit, she ordered a hearty sandwich, a fruit cup, and a bag of low-fat chips online. She asked the clerk to attach a note to the bag: *A gift from your shopper. :)*

Lynita would be proud of her. Clearing her head, Imani entered her study mode and concentrated on the consequences of food and health deserts in the inner cities and ways to combat them.

Although genetics play a role in a person developing diabetes and heart disease, some conditions are preventable with proper diets and exercise for a healthy lifestyle, especially in our youth.

Our statistics have shown that nutritious foods are not accessible, which is why some organizations are encouraging neighborhood food gardens as one way to combat poverty. More needs to be done. Getting youths involved will encourage them to spend time outdoors, which is a much-needed source of vitamin D. . . .

Imani hmphed. "All that sounds good, but some streets aren't even safe for children to walk to their schools." Imani tugged on a few strands of her hair, a telltale habit when she was deep in thought.

A text interrupted her—Brandon. **Hey, beautiful.**

She accepted his compliments, or maybe it was a flirt.

I received your lunch box. Thank you. My staff says I'm blushing.

Me too, she kept to herself.

Are you planning to shop soon?

Not yet. I need a couple more hours of reading so I can take this quiz before I leave. Imani had to pass on the first try, or she would lag behind. But after yesterday's scare, she had better get out sooner rather than later, hopefully before the sun set. **I'm glad you're in the business of getting people off the sofa.**

Her phone rang.

"Hi," Brandon said in a voice that was clear, deep, and confident. "*Mmm*. This loaded turkey sandwich is delicious, and the baked chips were what a hungry man needed. I don't want to distract you from your studies."

Too late, but she welcomed the interruption.

"I wanted to remind you, please don't hesitate to call me for backup."

Right. For more than a year, Imani had thought she was selective about where to deliver. Yet some undesirable customers slipped through the cracks. She never considered having a backup until she actually needed one. "I will."

"Do you promise?" he said.

So he trusted her? Imani lowered her lashes and savored his question. "Absolutely!"

Chapter 9

Brandon stared at the caller's name. Imani. She had never called him. It must be something big if she was taking time away from her studies. He nodded to his assistant to man the counter as he walked away for privacy.

"Good morning." Her voice had a ring to it. "My mom says if you come to our church on Sunday, she can arrange for you to speak with the seniors after the service."

"I'll be there." Brandon and Kyle had prayed for opportunities to get the word out about Time of Your Life. Their gyms offered a slower pace so that patrons would feel less intimidated by unrealistic goals.

He put the time and location into his phone notes. He had hoped to chat with her for a few moments, but Imani hurried off to study. Although Brandon respected her dedication, he struggled with patience when he wanted to hear her voice for at least two more minutes.

Less than four months away. That's how long Brandon counted until Imani graduated and he hoped there would be more time for them.

In preparation for his presentation, Brandon stopped by his barber's shop for a cut after work. He turned heads when he walked into work. Flirts from a group of eighty-something clients flattered him.

Although comfortable in his athletic gear, he knew how to dress to impress.

On Sunday morning, he paired a crisp brown shirt with a designer rust print tie. Black slacks and dress shoes completed his transformation.

When he strolled inside the foyer at Holy Ghost Power Temple, nothing prepared him for Imani Robinson.

The jeans, baseball cap, and sweater were gone. Imani was stunning in a colorful paisley dress that flattered her waistline and teased her knees. Where he easily towered over her when she wore her athletic shoes, today her heels brought her almost to eye level. And she was his focus as the white-and-gold background faded as he walked toward her.

Lovely without beauty enhancements, Imani was a showstopper with makeup that accentuated her brown eyes. Her hair bounced with curls. She smiled and reached for his hand. "Hi."

He accepted. Her fingers seemed softer than the night at the burger joint.

"You must be Brandon, from the way you're smiling at my daughter." An older version of Imani appeared, or maybe she had been beside her all along.

He released Imani's hand to shake her mother's. "Yes, ma'am."

"I'm Pauline Robinson." She smiled. "You're on time, a good quality. Let's get to our seats."

After the trio walked into the sanctuary, Brandon knelt at his seat and gave thanks for being in God's presence, then sat. He was amused that Pauline situated herself between him and Imani as if she were chaperoning teenagers.

The musicians led the congregation in an old hymn before the singers had everyone on their feet for more upbeat selections. Next, the pastor greeted guests and his members before opening his Bible.

"Saints, my message today is simple but important. We need Jesus for salvation, provision, and protection," Elder Durham said. "We don't see the demonic forces poised to destroy us, but God has sent angels to protect us. . . ."

Brandon and Imani exchanged secret glances. His mind captured the moment for safekeeping. Attraction replaced the fear that he remembered from that evening.

"Trust Him!" The preacher's words slapped Brandon back to attention. "The Lord told Jeremiah, 'I know the thoughts that I think toward you, thoughts of peace, and not of evil, to give you an expected end.' This promise came after Jeremiah prophesied the destruction of Jerusalem and the Jews being taken away captive to Babylon. But even in the darkest hour, God already has a plan of escape for us. Never forget that."

The sermon concluded forty minutes later, with Elder Durham urging the congregation to pray for one another. "For our faith to remain strong."

After the offering, the pastor asked Imani's mom to come to the pulpit with an important message.

"Praise the Lord, everyone. We have Brandon Johnson, owner of Time of Your Life Gym, here today to talk to the seasoned saints. Meet us in the dining hall after the benediction."

Imani walked beside him as they mingled with others on their way to the designated area. They didn't hold hands, but he felt their connection.

"Enjoy the message?" she asked.

"I did."

"Brandon, please feel welcome to come back again." Mrs. Robinson sneaked up between them. "My daughter has been deep in homework while in school, but soon that will be over, and she won't miss any Sundays, right, dear?" When Imani confirmed with a nod, her mother continued, "Brandon, tell me about your salvation walk," she said, looping her arms with his and Imani's.

He liked Pauline. She was direct. "When my parents died years ago, I was angry, but God showed me mercy and I surrendered, repented, was baptized in water in Jesus' name, and heard God speak through me with a heavenly language. I've let getting the business up and running come between me and my commitment to God on Sundays. I'll do better."

"Excellent."

There was a notable difference in crowd size from that in the sanctuary. The number of members shrank from a thousand to about fifty in the dining hall.

Imani sat in the front row next to her mom and gave Brandon a thumbs-up as he addressed the group.

"Hello, everyone. Again, my name is Brandon Johnson. My brother, Kyle, and I own Time of Your Life Gym. Our vision is to create a space where guests aged fifty and over can mingle while exercising. Most insurance plans cover our membership fee . . ." Brandon listed other amenities at his two locations that stirred interest, while folks nodded and chatted among themselves.

Pauline stood. "And I called my insurance company. They said I can get transportation to my sessions. You probably will too. If Brandon throws in some treats, we'll be there."

"Mom!" Imani tried to hush her.

"My staff and I will make sure you're safe and have nutritious snacks."

"Where can I sign up?" one gentleman asked, raising his hand.

Brandon was about to hand out the gym brochures when he realized he had left them in the car.

Imani stood and mouthed, "I have to go."

"I'll be right back," Brandon told his audience, then walked Imani to her car and retrieved the material from his. The sweet scent of her perfume tickled his nose. "Thanks for staying."

"What you're doing is important. The right types of food and moderate exercise are crucial components of public health," she said as she stumbled in her heels. But Brandon was there to steady her.

"I can't wait for our first real date." He linked his fingers through hers.

Imani nudged him. "I'm trying not to think about it."

Brandon feigned a pout.

"I mean, I do think about it, but with the time and money invested in this program, I want to excel and move into a new career." She giggled and lowered her voice. "But I can't wait either."

"I'm loving that answer." He opened her car door and watched her drive off.

Chapter 10

For two consecutive months, Brandon and Kyle had seen a steady increase in membership at Time of Your Life gyms. Brandon praised God and thanked Mrs. Robinson for the blessing.

Her commanding personality rallied others at the church and even in her neighborhood to join.

"I know you're trying to win over my daughter," she told him after completing her paperwork.

"I am." Brandon nodded.

Mrs. Robinson squinted and eyed him up and down. She looked fashionable in her color-coordinated sweatband, workout attire, and sneakers. "Then I hope to see you more at service."

Before he could respond, more of her church members walked inside, greeting him with their smiles and a church atmosphere of "Praise the Lord."

Throughout the day, Brandon's random thoughts of Imani made him lose his concentration. They had progressed from texts to morning calls. To respect her time, even if she protested, he limited their talks to ten minutes. He set a timer.

"It was crazy at the supermarkets yesterday with customers ordering items for Thanksgiving."

He listened as he inspected the equipment to make sure the area around it was clean, then the timer went off, and reluctantly, they said their goodbyes.

Kyle gave him a hard time because Brandon refused any interruptions while speaking with Imani. "I'm surprised you don't tag along and push Imani's shopping cart."

"Hmmm." Brandon rubbed his chin. "There's an idea."

"I was just jokin.'"

Wham echoed through the gym. Kyle and Brandon hurried to the weight area and reminded clients to increase their weights gradually. "We don't want you to strain your muscles by pushing yourself before your body can adapt," Brandon said.

"Or damage our equipment," Kyle added.

One evening, Brandon had just checked in at his North City location when Imani called him. She was in the checkout line for the next available checker.

"Hi, beautiful. Long lines?"

"Yep. How did you know?"

"Long lines are my best friend. I get to hear your voice."

Imani tsked. "Lines are the enemy for us because we're timed on everything, but the holidays are a madhouse. Shelves are thin, making it hard to replace some requested items. Butterscotch chips aren't a substitute for dark chocolate chips for cookies."

"Got a point." Brandon stopped at a red light. "Speaking of holidays, what are *we* doing for the holiday?" It was a bold request, but it was out there.

"*We're* sharing Thanksgiving if you accept my invitation to dine at my mom's house."

"That's a definite yes." His plans with Kyle and the family were officially canceled.

When he heard *"Proceed to register eleven"* in the background, Imani said, "Got to go."

So the countdown had begun. One month until her graduation and their first date.

FINALLY, A HOLIDAY Imani could enjoy. Her summer holidays had consisted of books with barbecues.

She spent the night at her mother's house to help prepare their Thanksgiving feast. Of course, Imani brought homework for later, but the day was about relaxing, eating, and enjoying family. Then there was Brandon. She was thrilled to spend time with him.

"You must be excited!" Lynita said when she stopped by to pick up the apple pie Imani's mother had baked for Lynita to take to work.

"I am. Who knew I would meet someone while delivering groceries? Tennis shoes instead of platforms, jeans instead of dress slacks, and T-shirts instead of flirty tops."

"I hope you were wearing a cap to protect yourself against the sunrays," Lynita said, giving free medical advice. In the kitchen, Lynita chatted with Imani's mom before she hugged them, then headed to the hospital to work her twelve-hour shift.

The next day, Imani opened the door and caught her breath. Brandon was dressed in a camel hat and a trench coat. His handsomeness was overpowering to her senses. Speechless, she moved back as he cleared the doorway. His stare, flared nostrils, and cologne commanded her attention.

"You look pretty." His voice was husky, then he cleared his throat. "Happy Thanksgiving. I brought homemade cookies courtesy of Aja and Tyler."

Exhaling, she thanked him and took the platter.

"Imani, take Brandon's coat and close the door. I feel a draft," her mother yelled from the kitchen.

"Sorry." Imani hoped she hid her blush as she remembered her manners, then led him to the kitchen.

Brandon and her mother had become buddies of sorts. Pauline often spilled the tea to Imani, giving a recap of her day at Brandon's gym and the hussies who tried to flirt with him. But her mother always reassured Imani that Brandon paid them no mind and she "shut them down."

Brandon kissed Pauline on the cheek.

Her mother praised the bakers' efforts as she tasted a cookie.

"Can I set the table, finish up, or do any heavy lifting?" Brandon asked.

"The table's set, food is ready, and I know you can bench-press Imani and me with little effort," she teased with mischief dancing in her eyes. "You're our guest. Relax and keep Imani company."

Brandon grinned. "I can do that."

Minutes later, dinner was served, and Brandon said grace. His prayer brought Imani to the brink of tears because it was so sincere.

After that, the conversation was as hearty as the dishes. Brandon kept the women amused with more of his niece and nephew's antics.

By the end of the evening, Imani accepted that love was on the sidelines for her and Brandon. Their attraction had accelerated from five to fifty since they met in the spring.

Judging from the smile on her mom's face, Pauline sensed it too.

Chapter 11

The kiss was everything. It held promise.

Imani would never forget it, as she and Brandon said goodnight on Thanksgiving. She was sure her mother was peeping from the kitchen.

It was short, sweet, and a tease.

Before bedtime, Imani thanked Jesus for His power to tame their hormones and resist temptation.

The next day, Black Friday was in full throttle. "Are you shopping today?" Brandon asked that morning when he called. He was already at work. "Gym membership usually surges this time of year until mid-February. People who overeat yesterday want to lose those pounds so they have space to pile them back on at Christmas."

Imani laughed. "Right. Yes, I'm taking advantage of folks who are at the malls and stores instead of at the grocery stores. But after today, it's crunch time—the final stretch to complete my thesis. I plan to spend the rest of the weekend at the library without distraction."

Brandon was quiet. "What if I bring you a snack after I leave church? You have to eat. What do you want?"

"Pizza." They laughed, but Brandon was the biggest distraction Imani had ever faced.

BRANDON WAS OVERWHELMED in a good way. The mad rush for fitness didn't let up at both gym locations. In the midst of the chaos, thoughts of Imani gave Brandon peace. He wanted her to succeed, not only selfishly so she would have time for him, but not be in harm's way again.

Since that first night when he'd trailed her to the dark neighborhood, she'd requested his bodyguard services only twice. He'd obliged without question.

Did you not know that My name is a strong tower and the righteous come to Me and are safe? God thundered. *I told you to pray for her, not take credit for her safety.*

Brandon felt sucker punched by God's reprimand, but the Lord was right. He repented.

On Sunday, Brandon sat in the same spot beside her mother at church and missed Imani's presence. The sermon "Feeding God's Sheep" resonated with him after the sumptuous meal he'd shared with the Robinsons on Thanksgiving.

"Folks and families are hungry year-round. The public's generosity spikes this time of year and then flatlines until the next holiday," Elder Durham said. He paused and rested a fist on his waist. "Wouldn't it be something if we fed families year-round? Pay for someone's groceries at the store on a Monday... just because. Deliver sandwiches or dinner to neighbors you never see on a Saturday, or treat a senior to lunch mid-week. The opportunities are endless to bless others so that they can hear the gospel. It shouldn't take a holiday for you to show the love of Christ. Never turn away someone who is hungry. Jesus didn't."

After saying bye to Mrs. Robinson and others, Brandon drove home, changed, and then put into practice what the pastor had preached.

At the store, Brandon grabbed a bouquet. While in the checkout lane, he purchased groceries for a woman in front of him and a man behind him. The woman declined because her bill totaled more than two hundred dollars. "Let me bless you so you can bless someone else."

Tears filled her eyes as she thanked him.

The older man wept openly. "Thank you, sir. Now I can buy my medicine."

Humbled, Brandon's heart ached for those who had little or nothing. "Lord, what more can I do? I can't feed everybody, so show me who you want me to bless." His heart was still heavy when he stopped at a local pizza shop and ordered four slices of beef pizza, side salads, and two lemonades.

Brandon turned into the university's campus and followed the signs to the J. Baker Library. He texted Imani: **Here with food. Where do I go?**

Fourth floor, she texted back.

Taking the roses and pizza, Brandon headed for the building. Inside the elevator, he pushed the button to the floor. When the doors opened, Imani was waiting for him.

Her eyes brightened as a smile welcomed him. Brandon wanted to drop everything in his hands and engulf her in his arms. Instead, he handed her the flowers and accepted a soft hug.

"How was service?" she asked while sniffing the bouquet.

"Thought-provoking. The sermon was on feeding God's sheep." Brandon trailed her to a private room enclosed with glass walls. It was the size of an extended walk-in closet. Her computer and papers were spread across a square wooden table. Four chairs were on each side.

"Tell me about the message while we eat, then I have to finish my paper." Imani made room for her roses and the food.

Shaking off his coat, Brandon nodded, then folded it over the back of the chair. He arranged the food, careful of her papers, and took a seat.

Brandon said grace, and they dug in.

"Mmm. This is so good."

He nodded, then took a sip of his drink. "Your pastor doesn't want our kindness to be limited to the holidays. We are to feed our neighbors or strangers in times of need." He shared some Scriptures. When the pizza, salad, and lemonade had vanished, he playfully ordered Imani back to the books.

Imani switched modes.

Stretching his legs, Brandon folded his arms, content to be in the same room with her. He studied her expressions and body language. She hummed, paused, then squinted at what she read.

Her beauty was God-given, and he tried not to stare at her lips and think of the brief kiss they'd shared on Thanksgiving night.

Imani began to doze. Blinking, she shifted in her seat or hummed, but it didn't recharge her. He scooted next to her. "Keep going. You got this." He squeezed her hand.

Looking at him, her eyes were suddenly alert. She bit her bottom lip, then cleared her throat. Brandon glanced at her monitor and began to read her paper and softly prayed for her.

"Amen." She leaned over and brushed her lips against his. "I'm ready now."

Chapter 12

one. Imani had successfully completed her coursework. Unknowingly, Brandon had given her the extra push to finish her paper. She submitted it to her professor to receive her master's degree.

Brandon. Imani had never experienced an emotion that she would classify as love, but it was indisputable that Brandon cared, and that made her happy.

Lynita said Imani glowed when they met for breakfast. "Tell me more." Lynita's eyes, tired from working overnight, were fully alert. She sipped her hot chocolate, then leaned forward for the details.

Imani's lips curled into a smile. "We haven't really gone out on a date, but every time we've seen each other, whether delivering groceries or at church, it's become a dating adventure. When I worked on my thesis, he brought food to the library and kept me company while I studied. At first, I was apprehensive because I thought he would be a distraction."

"Girl, from the photo you showed me, Brandon Johnson is."

Imani giggled as her mind wandered. "No, he's an attraction. He protected me, supported my goals, and honored my wishes to hold off on dating."

Lynita gave her a side-eye "And yet, he seemed to be always there."

"I know." Imani grinned widely. "When I began to doze at the library, Brandon sat next to me and encouraged me to keep reading. He read what I'd written and began to ask questions. That energized me, and I locked in."

"Does he have any more brothers?" Lynita anchored her elbow on the table and sighed.

"Nope. Just him and Kyle, who I can't wait to meet, because his children are as adorable as they are mischievous. But get this, as I reviewed my changes, I heard Brandon's faint snore."

Her mind recalled the moment. Brandon's expression had been peaceful, so Imani hadn't disturbed him. She had kissed his forehead and smiled. That tidbit she kept from her friend.

The following week, it was business as usual when Imani shopped for groceries. Since her tuition and graduation fees were paid, these earnings would be used as extra spending money.

The Friday before Christmas, she and Brandon braved the jungle of shoppers to get last-minute bargains for family and friends.

"Don't anybody buy online anymore?" Brandon huffed.

Imani nudged him. "I like getting out, seeing the colorful lights, listening to Christmas music playing in the stores, and giving to the Salvation Army and other charities I see along the way."

He nodded. "You're right. Ever since the sermon last month, I've been more conscious about giving, so when I order groceries, I purposefully buy extras to give to food banks."

She looked at him. "I like that idea." Imani felt like the drummer boy—girl. What could she give? As they roamed the ransacked aisles, Imani noticed five-, ten-, and twenty-dollar stocking stuffers on the end caps. She began to grab some. "I can give these to my customers when I deliver their orders."

Brandon rewarded her with a smile, but it was the expression on his face that made her blush. "I like the way you think. You're perfect for me."

Imani was speechless. Wow. She didn't know how to respond as Brandon began to collect a few stocking stuffers too.

Once they had a stockpile, the two searched for gift wrap, bows, and tape.

At the checkout, Brandon and Imani disagreed over who would pay for what.

A grouchy older Black man behind them lifted his voice. "Clearly, neither one of you has enough money. I'll buy it," he said to the clerk and handed her his card.

Imani and Brandon declined the man's offer, but he didn't back down until the cashier interrupted them. "You two are holding up my line." She arched a bushy brow. "Take your blessings."

Brandon shrugged. "God has a sense of humor."

Imani turned to their benefactor. "These are giveaways for random strangers, so you got in on the blessing, so thank you."

The man's grin was wide enough for a dental inspection. "Should we add more?"

"No!" the cashier joined the chorus of customers behind them.

Brandon and Imani rushed to load their purchases into their cart, waved at the gentleman, then headed for Brandon's vehicle.

Happiness swelled within Imani. She loved being with him. They had a natural flow together.

No pretense or friction.

Harmony.

"Hungry?" Brandon asked as he buckled his seatbelt.

"Yep. That was work back there stuffing those bags to fit in the back." She smiled.

"I don't see how you have the patience to wait in long lines to check out customers' orders again and again."

Imani scrunched her nose. "I won't miss that part."

After deciding on what to eat, Brandon drove to the Greek House. She stayed in the vehicle while he went inside to order them gyros and salads. She admired his walk. He moved with confidence, and when he wasn't in his sweats, everything he wore was a fashion statement.

Brandon returned with their food and grinned at her.

"What?" Imani couldn't help but return his smile.

"You make me smile." He shrugged and started the ignition.

"I feel like something is missing from our stocking stuffers." She scrolled through items on her phone as Brandon drove to her house. "Jesus needs to get the credit for what we're doing, or it's only commercial Christmas."

He nodded. "I agree, but what?"

"Perfect!" she said as she searched online for something inspirational. "Here are some tiny scrolls that have Scriptures on them, and if I place the order now with rush delivery, I'll have them in two to four hours."

"Do it."

Back at her house, Imani took the food into the kitchen. "Brandon, do you mind starting a fire?"

Her home might not be as elaborate as his, but one thing she loved about her smaller home was the natural fireplace.

With the flames building, Imani brought trays with the plated food and some silverware, and they sat in front of the fire.

Taking her hand, Brandon said grace. "Lord, I thank You for Your blessings in our lives. My business is booming, and Imani will start a new career. Thank You for putting it on our hearts to think about others, and we give thanks for our meal. Please bless the food and the hands that prepared it. And help us do our part to feed those who are hungry. In Jesus' name. Amen."

"Amen." She playfully scrunched her nose. "You came with a prayer list."

"I say whatever is on my heart."

And that's why the man has been genuine since the first day he prayed for me, she thought.

As the fire blazed, the miniature scrolls arrived, and the fun began as Imani played Christian Christmas songs from YouTube while they worked. She didn't mind the clutter in her living room as she and Brandon competed for the best-wrapped gifts. But tying ribbons around the tiny Scripture scrolls was challenging for both of them, but they managed to complete the task.

"You know what would really be fun?" he asked. She shook her head. "I want to be a personal shopper for a day with you."

"You think it's easy, huh?" Lifting a brow, Imani snickered. "Home Delivery times your speed per item, replacements, refunds, and chats with customers."

"I'm up for the challenge. I got this."

Chapter 13

On Saturday, Brandon got his wish. Imani agreed to let him accompany her on her last time as a personal shopper. A foreign concept until Brandon started using the service because he didn't want to take his niece and nephew to the store. He had usually made a list, stopped at the store after he left work, and cooked at home.

One day, a personal shopper changed his life—both personally and professionally.

Now, he prayed for the Lord to fulfill Imani's happiness. She hadn't heard back about the positions she'd applied for last week.

"It's the holidays. People are on vacation," he had said to reassure her the previous evening while they'd battled gift wrapping.

"I know."

What could make her smile? Flowers.

They had to be something unique for Imani. After searching online, he stumbled upon Franco's Flower Shop. He hoped the Pink Christmas Romance Ramo Buchon flowers would cheer her up. The shade reminded him of the lip gloss she had worn after they'd first met. Besides the pink and yellow roses, there were peppermint candy canes and male and female gingerbread cookies placed on top. The bouquet sat on top of pink and white napkins that reminded him of rose petals.

Hours later, when Imani opened the door, she was decked out in a red and white striped scarf around her neck like a peppermint for the final occasion. His nostrils inhaled the chilled air, then exhaled like smoke from a dragon. "Morning, beautiful. I'm reporting for duty."

She stared at the flowers and her jaw dropped. "These are incredible." She looked from them to him. "I've never seen anything like this before." She held the arrangement as if it were a baby.

Brandon hoped she would notice the cold smoke coming from his nose, a signal for her to join him.

"Oh, I'm sorry." She looped an arm through his and pulled him into her foyer. "Come in. Brandon, these are the most beautiful flowers I've ever seen." The amazement lingered on her face.

"I'm glad you like them."

Since they were already in a vase, she placed it on her table in front of the window, patted her cheek, then moved it across the room to the mantel. Shaking her head, she didn't like that setup.

Chuckling, Brandon lifted it. "The third time's a charm. Where to now, Miss Robinson?"

"I guess back on the table by the window. But I don't want it to get too much sun."

"It won't today. Looks like it might snow."

With her full attention, she blinked. "If that's so, we need to hurry and shop. I don't like delivering in bad weather."

Brandon waved his phone in the air. "I've decided to place a personal order to see if you will get it."

Imani squinted as Brandon helped her slip on her coat. "You do know that if another shopper snatches it first, you won't be home to accept your groceries."

"Hmm." He tapped his chin as they stepped outside. "Good point."

"When you place the order, mark your delivery as a 'drop off and take a picture.'"

"Got it." Brandon helped her into his SUV, then took his seat behind the steering wheel. Instead of driving off, he bit his bottom lip. "Okay, I'm about to do this."

He scrolled through his phone, adding items until Imani rested her hand over his.

"Brandon, this is my last day. We have a mission to bless others." She looked in the backseat, where two oversized trash bags were bulging with gifts. "This isn't about you stocking up for a catastrophe."

Giving her a salute, he tamed his excitement. "Right. I'll refocus. I'll go with what's in the cart. Are you signed into your app?"

"Yep. Go ahead. Place it."

Brandon tapped the button as if it would detonate his phone. They laughed at his silliness as they waited.

Orders dropped. Some were ridiculously low-paying. "That's not worth the gas to deliver them without a tip." She pointed at an eleven-dollar order. With their heads together, Imani explained why she wouldn't take them. "The pay on this one is an insult, given the large number of items they ordered, or this one that's a longer drive with little pay."

Suddenly, an order paying thirty-seven dollars, including tip, appeared.

Imani's fingers were fast. She claimed it. "I got it."

Brandon blinked. "You're good."

"It's yours," she said in disbelief, shaking her head. "But you're not getting any freebies from the bag." She waggled her finger.

"I got what I want right here," he said, starting the ignition and linking his fingers through hers, "let's get to work." He checked the rearview mirror, then took off. The simplicity of shopping with Imani was an experience that Brandon wouldn't pass up.

At the grocery store, Brandon wrapped his hands around the cart's handlebar with the excitement of a six-year-old ready to race, and the store aisles were his tracks. "How does this work?" He towered over her, sniffing her perfume that tickled his nose.

"Come on. Let me show you the ropes." Imani looped her arm through his. Maybe not professional behavior as a personal shopper, but Brandon loved it.

"I'm in a happy place with you." He whistled as they strolled down the aisle.

"Here are the crackers I wanted." Brandon was about to place them in the cart.

Imani took them out of his hand. "Not so fast." She scanned the barcode with her phone. "This helps me keep track of the items I've done and how many are left to do. See, the crackers disappeared from my screen."

Side hustle or not, Imani took it seriously. When he tried to add junk food to the cart, she gently scolded him.

The store was busy, and Brandon noticed an elderly couple who were overdressed for grocery shopping but seemed to be enjoying themselves.

"Awww. Look, honey. They are such a striking couple," the woman said to her husband, loud enough for Imani and Brandon to hear as they crossed paths.

When they met again in another aisle, the same woman stopped them. Her eyes twinkled.

"Excuse me, honey. You two are so cute together. I don't see a ring. What are you waiting on, young man?" She jutted her chin out and squinted at Brandon.

The woman had no idea that he had been waiting for this very moment to explore a relationship with Imani. Even his niece and nephew had started to call Imani "the grocery lady." It seemed like everyone was rooting for them, even strangers.

"Oh, no." Imani shook her head. "I'm his personal shopper."

"And I'm her bodyguard." Brandon wiggled his brow and mumbled, "For now."

Chapter 14

Imani, with Brandon's assistance, completed his order in record time. Before they drove off, she entered his address into her navigation for fun.

He jokingly grunted. "I know my way to my own house."

"We'll see," she teased him. "You wanted to experience a day in the life of a personal shopper, and that's what I'm doing."

"Okay, I'll play along." He attentively followed the navigation.

"You have reached your destination," it said ten minutes later.

"Put on your hazard lights, and let's get your bags." She was about to open the door, but Brandon stopped her.

"I can get the bags. It's fun and games up to this point, but that's on pause. I'm opening your door. That isn't negotiable."

"Okay," she said in a soft voice.

When Brandon unlocked his front door to take the groceries inside, she stopped him, shaking her head. "We're back in professional mode again. Since your delivery is tagged as a drop-off, we have to place them on the porch first, so I can take a photo and complete the delivery."

Then the orders kept coming in, and Imani wasn't as picky about accepting them. She had Brandon with her.

Imani showed him her system for shopping for three orders simultaneously. "Customer A is baking. She's getting powdered sugar, almond flour, shelled nuts, and other ingredients."

"The man could be the chef too. Just sayin'." He looked away and whistled.

Shopping with Brandon would definitely slow her down. "Customer B may have overnight guests because of the waffles, French toast, bacon, sausage, various flavors of juice, and milk."

"Okay," Brandon stopped her. "Let me guess about Customer C, who is probably prepping for the company, based on the cleaning supplies. Evidently, the reward is Christmas cookies, eggnog, and chips."

They laughed. "You can tell a lot about a person by what they eat," she said.

At the register, Brandon asked, "How did we do?"

"We beat our time, but we can't slow down. We have a lot of gifts for customers."

Brandon kept the items separated as he loaded up the bags for delivery. First stop, Customer A, had four bags. Brandon took them, and she trailed with the gifts. "You know, I think the groceries may be lighter than these toys from Santa's workshop stunt."

All three customers' instructions were to drop off orders. She and Brandon rummaged through the bag of gifts. She pulled out a small box that likely contained a Burt's Bees Everyday Beauty Set, hoping the customer was a woman, and placed it on top of the grocery bags.

They did their second drop-off. Brandon pulled a regular gift box and added it to the bags on the porch.

As Imani walked back to the vehicle, she paused and stared at the next-door property, where uncut grass from the fall held piles of leaves hostage. Oil stains blemished the driveway and made the house an eyesore on the block, but two worn children's bikes caught her attention.

Brandon came to her side. "What's wrong?"

"I think that homeowner needs a blessing." She pointed and looked at him for confirmation.

He walked back to his vehicle and reached into the bag until his arm disappeared inside. "Too bad we didn't mark the gifts, but I know we got a couple of coloring book packs with crayons."

Brandon frowned. "After the next delivery, do you think we can go grocery shopping for them?" she suggested.

She agreed with him.

After the last two deliveries, they returned to the grocer's and shopped. As they began to check out, Brandon wouldn't let Imani buy anything. "After today, you're unemployed, so keep your money." He turned to the clerk. "I would like to get a one-hundred-dollar gift card."

Imani gasped, about to protest. "Can you afford that? But isn't your business struggling?"

"We're doing better than projected. Prayers and your mom changed things. Thanks for being concerned." His eyes showed adoration.

She hoped her eyes reflected the same emotion. How did the women at the gym and others let Brandon slip through their fingers? His generosity extended beyond his wallet. His thoughtfulness was like a warm embrace.

"Kyle and I don't dip into our business funds. This is my money I'm spending. Plus, I'm happy to report that both gym locations have waiting lists. . . and added Kyle and I added early morning classes for early risers," he said, handing the cashier his credit card.

Wow. All that mattered was that Brandon had reached his goal. Imani stifled a sigh. All she needed was a job offer after the holidays.

"Hey, what's on your mind?" he asked as she helped him load up the groceries. He stopped and gave her his full attention, waiting for her answer.

Imani shrugged. "Hoping I get the job I really want at the agency."

He put his arm around her shoulder and pulled her closer to his chest. "God's listening."

"I know." Imani bobbed her head. "Thanks for the reminder. We'd better get going. The temperature is dropping."

"Do you remember the house?" he asked.

She scrolled through the addresses on her phone. "I think it was Nelson Lane. The 6700 block."

Once Brandon was behind the wheel, he followed the navigation's directions. Soon, the neighborhood eyesore made its presence known as he turned the corner. Brandon and Imani had chosen a variety of food options for the family, including fun, essential, and dessert items. Clutching the bags in their arms, the two fell into step toward the porch. "Hey, the gifts I placed here from earlier are gone," she said.

"That means they're home." He positioned the bags near the door while Imani returned to the trunk for more gifts.

"Should we ring the doorbell?" she whispered. "There are perishable items."

They didn't have to, as the door swung open. A fair-skinned man, age undetermined, with thinning hair and dressed in overalls, frowned at them. "I didn't order this stuff. Take it back."

A little girl came to the door and looked at the bags. "Are you Santa's helpers?" Her eyes grew large.

"No," Imani shook her head, "we're God's helpers, and we bought you some food."

The little girl jumped in place. "I'm hungry, Grandpa!"

The man seemed embarrassed, then stood taller as if he was about to reject it.

Imani silently prayed for him to take the food.

"Sir," Brandon said, "we can't take it back to the store. If you know someone who is hungry, this is for them." He reached into his pocket and pulled out the gift card, and urged the man to take it. "Merry Christmas." He took Imani's hand and guided her down the stairs without looking back.

"You think we did the right thing?" Imani whispered. "He didn't look too grateful."

"It was a front. There were times when I wasn't grateful for my parents' help, but later I learned to accept it if I wanted to succeed. That grandpa took the small gifts we left earlier. He'll take the food and have a good Christmas."

In his vehicle, Imani scrolled through her phone, where orders were endless like corn in a field. "I just accepted two orders, and the deliveries are close to the store."

Brandon nodded. Instead of heading back to their destination, he did a U-turn and slowly crept past the house they'd just left. The grandpa was picking up the last of the groceries. Brandon grinned. "Come on, let's make someone else's Christmas bright."

Chapter 15

C*hristmas Eve*

Brandon didn't want to take anything for granted. His dinner date with Imani had to be everything.

God had sent Imani to his door as his blessing. Imani was still waiting for hers in the form of a job offer.

I'm faithful, God whispered.

"Yes, You are, Lord," Brandon said. Whatever the Lord said, Jesus was good for it.

Time of Your Life had seen an increase in gym memberships. The church's seniors engaged more in socializing on Mondays, Wednesdays, and Fridays than they did in exercising. But their presence was about more than the revenue; they changed the atmosphere.

Brandon grunted, surprised at the nervousness he couldn't explain. Tying his tie, he studied his reflection in the closet's full-length mirror.

It was time. He donned his hat and coat, then jiggled his keys in one hand and scooped up Imani's Christmas gift in the other, which his sister-in-law helped him pick out.

The snowfall, which had been predicted three days ago, had come as Brandon drove to Imani's house. "Perfect."

The streets dazzled with Christmas lights strung from one tree to the next. A few days ago, Brandon had left work to help decorate Imani's house.

He placed the box on the passenger seat and smiled, recalling when Aja walked in on them while they were in front of the computer.

"Mommy, what are you and Uncle Brandon doing?"

"Buying a gift for Imani."

"Is it a ring?" she asked earnestly as two pairs of eyes stared at her.

"Not yet." Brandon chuckled as he shooed his niece out of the home office at their house.

Before Brandon could park the car, Imani stood in the doorway, as he had done many times, waiting for her delivery. His mind captured the image of the blowing snow swirling at her feet and the glow from her gold dress.

Brandon stepped out and crushed the snow under his feet to get to her. The weather wasn't slowing them down.

She reached out and guided him into the house. "I've got news." Her eyes glittered.

"You got the job," he said, hoping he was right.

"Yes, I start on January 5th." She twirled around, dancing with a silent partner until Brandon joined her. They both laughed.

"We'd better go. We have a reservation on the rooftop at Park Place." When she gave him a doubtful look, Brandon explained, "It's enclosed in the winter."

"Oh." She exhaled, patting her chest. "That would have been memorable once I thawed."

"But first open your gift." He handed her the box.

She studied the wrapping, then eyed him curiously. When she lifted the lid, she sucked in her breath. "A charm bracelet. I never had one. And it's Afrocentric." She fingered the rhinestone-covered letters that spelled diva and crown from the Small Sisters Shop. Brandon was sold when he saw the cutout shape of a rhinestone heart and a pink lipstick inside.

"It's perfect!" She handed it to him to wrap around her slender wrist, which was soft and delicate.

When he finished, she rested her head on his chest and hugged him. Brandon trapped her in his arms.

It was torture. Brandon didn't want to rush the moment, but they had to leave. "Imani?"

"Hmmm." She squeezed tighter and sighed. "This is what won me over that night you trailed me. No words or chastening, but the comfort that a hug could give. Thank you." She looked up and they kissed.

That, he did not rush.

IMANI WAS HAPPY. A snow drift seemed to create a thin red carpet effect from her door to Brandon's vehicle. When he opened her door, gift boxes of various shapes and sizes were on the seat.

"What is all this?" She didn't recognize any of the gift paper they had used.

"I call it Imani's Spa Collection, because each box has everything you need to relax."

"Aww, thank you." She brushed her lips on his.

Brandon got inside and then reached into the back for a basket to place the boxes in. She loved the idea.

The snow had stopped by the time a valet greeted them at the Met Square Building downtown, which housed a mix of business, residential, and retail space, with most of the shopping concentrated on the top floors.

Excited, Imani squeezed Brandon's hand. His presence made her feel protected, not just physically but emotionally, as they strolled through the lobby to the elevator, where Brandon pushed the button for the forty-second floor. Inside, they embraced until their ride came to a stop on the top floor.

The doors opened to an unimaginable world of Christmasland where eight-foot Nutcracker figurines stood at attention, almost startling Imani. Brandon's hand around her waist reminded her of his presence. After stepping out of the elevator, they passed gingerbread house villages and Christmas tree forests lavished with gold, silver, and red tinsel. At the end of the path were two male hosts dressed as toy soldiers.

"This is incredible," she whispered.

"Good evening. You have reservations?"

"Yes." Brandon gave them his name, then he and Imani followed one of the toy soldiers to a table near the edge of the enclosed rooftop.

Brandon removed her coat, then pulled out her chair. He took off his own and sat across from her.

"This view is incredible. With the snow on the rooftops, it looks like a sleepy town waiting for Santa."

"Yep, while we're waiting for the Lord to return."

"I never want to forget that Jesus is the reason for the season," she said as Brandon reached for her hand and smiled at her nails. She had waited in a packed nail salon yesterday for the results he admired today.

Two children dressed as elves approached their table to take their orders. Clearly, the older child was prompting the younger, shy one to talk.

"Hello, our spesh-tees tonight are stuffed turkey. He's dead, so he won't run away. . . ."

Using all their willpower not to laugh, Imani and Brandon listened politely as the child gave them the option of a turkey that wouldn't run away, road lamb leg—meaning roasted leg of lamb—and a slow cooker basket, which Imani guessed was probably a brisket. When the boy finished, the girl recited the drinks.

"We have eggnog," she leaned closer, "and it really has eggs they didn't cook. Yuk." She scrunched her nose. "We have sparkling ginger and wine. Mommy has to bring you the wine."

Imani nodded. "Well, I'll have the sparkling ginger ale."

"Me too," Brandon said.

Once the elves were out of view, he and Imani faced the window and released their laughter until their bellies ached.

"They are so cute."

Instead of turkey, they decided on the leg of lamb and the sides. "Any discussion of gyms and shopping is off the table tonight. Can we talk about 'us'? Because I really would like there to be an us." Brandon rested his hands on hers again.

"Me too." So the two of them shared their pet peeves, hobbies, and favorite colors.

Brandon talked about his passion for trying healthy recipes and cycling. "One thing I do thank God for is steering me back into church." Closing his eyes, he chuckled. "Your mother quizzes me on key points from the sermons when she comes in."

"That is my mom."

When the bell tolled at midnight, they shared a Christmas kiss that was sweet, slow like a cooker, and a promise that it would be an "us" for a long time.

The End

About the Author

Pat Simmons is a multi-published Christian romance author of forty-plus titles. She is a self-proclaimed genealogy sleuth passionate about researching her ancestors and casting them in starring roles in her novels. She is a five-time recipient of the RSJ Emma Rodgers Award for Best Inspirational Romance: *Still Guilty, Crowning Glory, The Confession, Christmas Dinner*, and *Queen's Surrender (To A Higher Calling)*. Pat's first inspirational women's fiction, *Lean On Me*, with Sourcebooks, was the national library system's February/March Together We Read Digital Book Club pick. *Here for You* and *Stand by Me* are also part of the Family is Forever series. Her holiday indie release, *Christmas Dinner*, and traditionally published, *Here for You*, were featured in *Woman's World*, a national magazine. *Here for You* was also listed in the "7 Great Reads That Help to Keep the Faith" by Sisters From AARP. She contributed an article, "I'm Listening," in the *Chicken Soup for the Soul: I'm Speaking Now* (2021). Pat is the recipient of the 2022 Leslie Esdaile "Trailblazer" Award given by Building Relationships Around Books Readers' Choice for her work in the Christian fiction genre.

As a Christian, Pat describes the evidence of the gift of the Holy Ghost as a life-altering experience. She has been a featured speaker and workshop presenter at various venues nationwide. Pat has converted her sofa-strapped sports fanatic husband into an amateur travel agent, untrained bodyguard, GPS-guided chauffeur, and administrative assistant who is constantly on probation. They have a son and a daughter. Pat holds a B.S. in Mass Communications from Emerson College in Boston, Massachusetts, and has worked in radio, television, and print media for over twenty years. She oversaw the media publicity for the annual RT Booklovers Conventions for fourteen years. Visit her at www.patsimmons.net[1].

---

1.   http://www.patsimmons.net

Other Christian Titles

The Jamieson Legacy
Book 1: Guilty of Love
Book 2: Not Guilty of Love
Book 3: Still Guilty
Book 4: The Acquittal
Book 5: Guilty by Association
Book 6: The Guilt Trip
Book 7: Free from Guilt
Book 8: Sandra Nicholson's Backstory
Book 9: The Confession
Book 10: The Guilty Generation
Book 11: Queen's Surrender (To a Higher Calling)
Book 12: Contempt: Grandma BB's Shenanigans
Book 13: Christmas Takeover (The Next Generation)
Book 14: Accomplices in Love (The Next Generation)
The Intercessors
Book 1: Day Not Promised
Book 2: Day She Prayed
Book 3: Days Are Coming
Book 4: Day of Salvation
The Carmen Sisters
Book 1: No Easy Catch
Book 2: In Defense of Love

Book 3: Driven to Be Loved
Book 4: Redeeming Heart
Love at the Crossroads
Book 1: Stopping Traffic
Book 2: A Baby for Christmas
Book 3: The Keepsake
Book 4: What God Has for Me
Book 5: Every Woman Needs a Praying Man
Restore My Soul
Book 1: Crowning Glory
Book 2: Jet: The Back Story
Book 3: Love Led by the Spirit
Family is Forever
Book 1: Lean on Me
Book 2: Here For You
Book 3: Stand by Me
Making Love Work Anthology
Book 1: Love at Work
Book 2: Words of Love
Book 3: A Mother's Love
God's Gifts
Book 1: Couple by Christmas
Book 2: Prayers Answered by Christmas
Perfect Chance at Love series
Book 1: Love by Delivery
Book 2: Late Summer Love
Single titles
Talk to Me
Her Dress

House Calls for the Holidays (short story)
Christmas Dinner
Christmas Greetings
Shopping for Christmas
Taye's Gift
Waiting for Christmas
House Calls for the Holidays
Anderson Brothers
Book 1: Love for the Holidays (Three novellas):
A Christian Christmas
A Christian Easter
A Christian Father's Day
Book 2: A Woman After David's Heart (A Valentine's Day Story)
Book 3: A Noelle for Nathan

IN *Crowning Glory*, Cinderella had a prince; Karyn Wallace has a King. While Karyn served four years in prison for an unthinkable crime, she embraced salvation through the Crowns for Christ outreach ministry. After her release, Karyn remains strong and confident, despite society's stigma against ex-offenders. Since Christ strengthens the underdog, Karyn refuses to stray from the scripture, "He whom the Son has set free is free indeed." Levi Tolliver, for the most part, is a practicing Christian. One contradiction is that he doesn't believe in turning the other cheek. He's steadfast in his belief that there is a price to pay for every sin committed, especially after the untimely death of his wife during a robbery. Then Karyn enters Levi's life. He is enthralled by her beauty and sweet spirit until he learns about her incarceration. If Levi can accept that Christ paid Karyn's debt in full, then a treasure awaits him. This is a powerful tale that reminds readers of the permanence of redemption.

Jet: The Back Story to Love Led By the Spirit, to say Jesetta "Jet" Hutchens issues is an understatement. In Crowning Glory, Book 1 of the Restoring My Soul series, she releases a firestorm of anger with an unforgiving heart. But every hurting soul has a history. In Jet: The Back Story to Love Led by the Spirit, Jet doesn't know how to cope with losing her younger sister, Diane. But God sets her on the road to a spiritual recovery. Jesus sends the handsome and single Minister Rossi Tolliver to guide her to ensure she doesn't get lost. Psalm 147:3 says Jesus can heal the brokenhearted and bind up their wounds. That sets the stage for Love Led by the Spirit.

In Love Led By the Spirit, Minister Rossi Tolliver is ready to settle down. Besides the outward attraction, he desires a sweet, humble woman who loves church folks. It sounds simple enough on paper, but when he gets off his knees, praying for that special someone to come into his life, God opens his eyes to the woman who has been there all along. There is only a slight problem. Love is the farthest thing from Jesetta "Jet" Hutchens' mind. But Rossi, the man and the minister, is hard to resist. Is Jet ready to allow the Holy Spirit to lead her to love?

IN *Stopping Traffic*, Book 1, Candace Clark has a phobia about crossing the street, and for a good reason. As fate would have it, her daughter's principal assigns her to crossing guard duties as part of the school's Parent Participation program. With no choice in the matter, Candace begrudgingly accepts her stop sign and safety vest, then reports to her designated crosswalk. Once Candace is determined to overcome her fears, God opens the door for a blessing, and Royce Kavanaugh enters her life, a firefighter built to rescue any damsel in distress. When a spark of attraction ignites, Candace and Royce soon discover more than one way to stop traffic.

In *A Baby For Christmas*, Book 2, yes, diamonds are a girl's best friend, but in Solae Wyatt-Palmer's case, she desires something more valuable. Captain Hershel Kavanaugh is a divorcee and the father of two adorable little boys. Solae has never been married and longs to be a mother. Although Hershel showers her with expensive gifts, his hesitation about proposing causes Solae to walk and never look back. As the holidays approach, Hershel must convince Solae she has everything he could ever want for Christmas.

In *The Keepsake*, Book 3, Until Death Us Do Part...or until Desiree walks away. Desiree "Desi" Bishop is devastated when she finds evidence of her husband's affair. God knew she didn't get married to one day have to stand before a judge and file for a divorce. But Desi wants out no matter how much her heart says to forgive Michael. That isn't easier said than done. She sees God's one acceptable reason for a divorce as the only opt-out clause in her marriage. Michael Bishop is a repenting man who loves his wife of three years. If only...he had paid attention to the red flags God sent to keep him from falling into the devil's snares. But Michael didn't and fell. Although God forgives him instantly when he repents, Desi's forgiveness moves at a snail's pace. After all the tears have been shed and forgiveness granted and received, the couple learns that some marriages are worth keeping.

In *What God Has For Me*, Book 4, pregnant or not, Halcyon Holland is leaving her boyfriend. When her ex makes no attempts to reconcile their relationship, Halcyon begins to second-guess whether or not she compromised her chance for a happily ever after. But Zachary Bishop has had his eye on Halcyon since he first saw her. What one man doesn't cherish, Zach is ready to treasure. He's on a mission to offer her a second chance at love that she can't refuse: unconditional love for a ready-made family. Halcyon will soon learn that her past circumstances won't hinder the Lord's blessings for them.

In *Every Woman Needs A Praying Man*, Book 5, first impressions can make or break a business deal, and they definitely could be a relationship buster, but an ill-timed panic attack draws two strangers together. Unlike firefighters who run into danger, instincts tell businessman Tyson Graham to be weary of a certain damsel in distress and run. Days later, the same woman struts through his door for a job interview. Monica Wyatt might possess the outward beauty and the brains on paper, but Tyson doesn't trust her to work for his firm, or maybe he doesn't trust his heart around her.

IN *Guilty of Love*, when do you know the most important decision of your life is the right one? Reaping the seeds from what she's sown, Cheney Reynolds moves into a historic neighborhood in Ferguson, Missouri, and becomes a reclusive. Her first neighbor, the incomparable Mrs. Beatrice Tilley Beacon aka Grandma BB, is an opinionated childless widow. Grandma BB is a self-proclaimed expert on topics Cheney isn't seeking advice—everything from landscaping to hip-hop dancing to romance. Then there is Parke Kokumuo Jamison VI, a direct descendant of a royal African tribe. He learned his family ancestry, African history, and lineage preservation before he could count. Unwittingly, they are drawn to each other, but it takes Christ to weave their lives into a spiritual bliss while He exonerates their past indiscretions.

In *Not Guilty*, one man, one woman, one God, and one big problem. Malcolm Jamieson wasn't the man who got away, but the man God instructed Hallison Dinkins to set free. Instead of their explosive love affair leading them to the wedding altar, God diverted Hallison to the prayer altar during her first visit back to church in years. Malcolm was convinced his woman had lost her mind to break off their engagement. Didn't Hallison know that Malcolm, a tenth-generation descendant of a royal African tribe, couldn't be replaced? Once Malcolm concedes that their relationship can't be savaged, he issues Hallison his edict, "If we're meant to be with each other, we'll find our way back. If not, that means there's a love stronger than we had." His words haunt Hallison until she begins to regret their breakup, and that's where their story begins. Someone has to retreat, and God never loses a battle.

In *Still Guilty*, Cheney Reynolds Jamieson made a choice years ago that is shaping her future and the future of the men she loves. A botched abortion prevented her from carrying a baby to term, and her husband, Parke K. Jamison VI, is expected to produce heirs. With a wife who cannot give him a child, Parke vows to find and get custody of his illegitimate son by any means necessary. Meanwhile, Cheney's twin brother, Rainey, struggles with his anger over his ex-girlfriend's actions that haunt him, and their father, Dr. Roland Reynolds, fights to keep an old secret in the past.

In *The Acquittal*, two worlds apart, but their hearts dance to the same African drum beat. On a professional level, Dr. Rainey Reynolds is a competent, highly sought-after orthodontist. Inwardly, he needs to be set free from the chaos of revelations that make him question if happiness is obtainable. To escape the drama, Rainey is willing to leave the country under the guise of a mission trip with Dentist Without Borders. Will changing his surroundings change him? If one woman can heal his wounds, then he will believe that there is really peace after the storm.

Ghanaian beauty Josephine Abena Yaa Amoah returns to Africa after completing her studies as an exchange student in St. Louis, Missouri. Although her heart bleeds for his peace, she knows she must step back and pray for Rainey's surrender to Christ so God can acquit him of his self-inflicted mental torture. In the Motherland of Ghana, Africa, Rainey not only visits the places of his ancestors but also embraces the liberty that Christ's Blood does to set every man free.

In *Guilty By Association*, how important is a name? To the St. Louis Jamiesons, tenth-generation descendants of a royal African tribe—everything. To the Boston Jamiesons, whose father never married their mother, there is no loyalty or legacy. Kidd Jamieson suffers from the "angry" male syndrome because his father was absent in the home but insisted his two sons carry his last name. It takes an old woman who mingles genealogy truths and Bible verses together for Kidd to realize his worth as a strong black man. He learns it's not his association with the name that identifies him, but the man he becomes that defines him.

In *The Guilt Trip*, Aaron "Ace" Jamieson lives carefree. He's good-looking and respectable when in the mood, but his weakness is women. If a woman tries to ambush him with a pregnancy, he takes off in the other direction. It's a lesson learned from his absentee father that responsibility is optional. Talise Rogers has a bright future ahead of her. She's pretty and has no problem catching a man's eye, which is exactly what she does with Ace. Trapping Ace Jamieson is the furthest thing from Talise's mind when she learns she is pregnant, and Ace rejects her. "I want nothing from you Ace, not even your name." And Talise meant it.

In *Free From Guilt*, it's salvation round-up time, and Cameron Jamieson's name is on God's hit list. Although his brothers and cousins embraced God—thanks to the women in their lives—the two-degreed MIT graduate isn't letting any woman take him down that path without a fight. He's satisfied with his career, social calendar, and good genes. But God uses a beautiful messenger, Gabrielle Dupree, to show him that he's in a spiritual deficit. Cameron learns that man's wisdom is like foolishness to God. For every philosophical argument he throws her way, Gabrielle exposes him to Scriptures that make him question his worldly knowledge.

In *Sandra Nicholson's Backstory*, Sandra has made good and bad choices throughout the years, but the best one was to give her life to Christ when her sons were small and to rear them up in the best Christian way she knew how. That was thirty-something years ago and Sandra has evolved from a young single mother of two rambunctious boys: Kidd and Ace Jamieson, to a godly woman seasoned with wisdom. Despite the challenges and trials of rearing two strong-willed personalities, Sandra maintained her sanity through the grace of God, which kept gray strands at bay. But there is something to be said about a woman's first love. Kidd and Ace Jamieson's father, Samuel Jamieson, broke their mother's heart. Can Sandra recover? Her sons don't believe any man is good enough for her, especially their absent father. Kidd doesn't deny his mother should find love again since she never married Samuel. But will she fall for a carbon copy of his father? God's love gives second chances.

In *The Confession*, Sandra Nicholson had made good and bad choices throughout the years, but the best one was to give her life to Christ when her sons were small and to rear them up in the best Christian way she knew how. That was thirty-something years ago and Sandra has evolved from a young single mother of two rambunctious boys, Kidd and Ace Jamieson to a godly woman seasoned with wisdom. Despite the challenges and trials of rearing two strong-willed personalities, Sandra maintained her sanity through the grace of God, which kept gray strands at bay.

Now, Sandra Nicholson is on the threshold of happiness, but Kidd believes no man is good enough for his mother, especially if her love interest could be a man just like his absentee father.

In *The Guilty Generation*, seventeen-year-old Kami Jamieson is so over being daddy's little girl. Now that she has captured the attention of Tango, the bad boy from her school, Kami's love for her family and God have taken a backseat to her teen crush. Although the Jamiesons have instilled godly principles in Kami since she was young, they will stop at nothing, including prayer and fasting, to protect her from falling prey to society's peer pressure. Can Kami survive her teen rebellion, or will she be guilty of dividing the next generation?

In *Queen's Surrender (To a Higher Calling)*, Opposites attract...or clash. The Jamieson saga continues with the Queen of the family in this inspirational romance. She's the mistress of flirtation, but Philip is unaffected by her charm. The two enjoy a harmless banter about God's will versus Queen's, who prefers her own free-will lifestyle. Philip doesn't judge her choices—most of the time—and Queen respects his opinions—most of the time. It's perfect harmony sometimes. Queen, the youngest sister of the Jamieson clan, wears her name as if it's a crown. She's single, sassy, and most of the time, loving her status, but she's about to strut down an unexpected spiritual path. Evangelist Philip Dupree is on the hot seat as the trial pastor at Total Surrender Church. The stalemate: They want a family man to lead their flock. The board's ultimatum is enough to make him quit the ministry. But can a man of God walk away from his calling? Can two people with different lifestyles and priorities cross paths and continue the journey as one? Who is going to be the first to surrender?

In *Contempt (Grandma BB's Shenanigans)*, Grandma BB, the unofficial matriarch of the Jamieson clan, is getting her house for the perfect homegoing celebration. After all, she's eighty-something. She summons Parke Jamieson VI, his brothers, cousins, and their families to participate in the practice funeral program—only if they follow her instructions. Since the Jamiesons are at her house with bodyguards Chip and Dale, they might have an impromptu family game night. The evening is full of surprises, especially when an unexpected visitor shows up to steal the show. With more work that needs to be done, Grandma BB plans to put her funeral on hold and stick around for a couple more generations.

In *Accomplices in Love*, Parke "Pace" Jamieson VIII knows something is special about Harmony Reed, his sister's college friend who was almost stranded in St. Louis for Christmas. She checks all his compatibility boxes: looks, charm, a great sense of humor, and intense attraction. Plus, the Jamiesons love her.

When not at school, Harmony lives in Chicago with her three overprotective brothers. She is not interested in a relationship with her best friend's brother.

Pace, who lives in St. Louis, is not deterred by the distance, her objections, or her brothers. He's a Jamieson, and they play to win.

In *Fun and Games with the Jamieson Men*, The Jamieson Legacy series inspired this game book of fun activities:• Brain Teasers• Crossword Puzzles• Word Searches •Sudoku •Mazes •Coloring Pages. The Jamiesons are fictional characters that emphasize Black Heritage, including Black American History tidbits, African American genealogy, and strong Black families. Relax, grab a pencil and play along.

THE CARMEN SISTERS SERIES

IN *No Easy Catch*, Book 1, Shae Carmen hasn't lost her faith in God, only the men she's come across. Shae's recent heartbreak was discovering that her boyfriend was not only married, but on the verge of reconciling with his estranged wife. Humiliated, Shae begins to second guess herself as why she didn't see the signs that he was nothing more than a devil's decoy masquerading as a devout Christian man. St. Louis Outfielder Rahn Maxwell finds himself a victim of an attempted carjacking. The Lord guides him out of harms' way by opening the gunmen's eyes to Rahn's identity. The crook instead becomes an infatuated fan and asks for Rahn's autograph, and as a goodwill gesture, directs Rahn out of the ambush! When the news media gets wind of what happened with the baseball player, Shae's television station lands an exclusive interview. Shae and Rahn's chance meeting sets in motion a relationship where Rahn not only surrenders to Christ, but pursues Shae with a purpose to prove that good men are still out there. After letting her guard down, Shae faces another scandal that rocks her world. This time the stakes are higher. Not only is her heart on the line, so is her professional credibility. She and Rahn are at odds as how to handle it and friction erupts between them. Will she strike out at love again? The Lord shows Rahn that nothing happens by chance and everything is done for Him to get the glory.

In *Defense of Love*, Book 2, nothing in Garrett Nash's life has made sense lately. When two people close to the U.S. Marshal wrong him deeply, Garrett expects God to remove them from his life. Instead, the Lord relocates Garrett to another city to start over, as if he were the offender instead of the victim. Criminal attorney Shari Carmen is comfortable in her own skin—most of the time. Being a "dark and lovely" African-American sister has its challenges, especially when it comes to relationships. Although she's a fireball in the courtroom, she knows how to fade into the background and keep the proverbial spotlight off her personal life. But literal spotlights are a different matter altogether. While playing tenor saxophone at an anniversary party, she grabs the attention of Garrett Nash. And as God draws them closer together, He makes another request of Garrett, one to which it will prove far more difficult to say "Yes, Lord."

In *Redeeming Heart*, Book 3, Landon Thomas (In Defense of Love) brings a new definition to the word "prodigal," as in prodigal son, brother or anything else imaginable. It's good that God's love covers a multitude of sins, but He isn't letting Landon off easy. His journey from riches to rags proves to be humbling and a lesson well learned. Real Estate Agent Octavia Winston is a woman on a mission, whether it's God's or hers professionally. One thing is for certain, she's not about to compromise when it comes to a Christian mate, so why did God send a homeless man to steal her heart? Minister Rossi Tolliver (Crowning Glory) knows how to minister to God's lost sheep and through God's redemption, the game changes for Landon and Octavia.

In *Driven to Be Loved*, Book 4, on the surface, Brecee Carmen has nothing in common with Adrian Cole. She is a pediatrician certified in trauma care; he is a transportation problem solver for a luxury car dealership (a.k.a., a car salesman). Despite their slow but steady attraction to each other, neither one of them are sure that they're compatible. To complicate matters, Brecee is the sole unattached Carmen when it seems as though everyone else around her—family and friends—are finding love, except her. Through a series of discoveries, Adrian and Brecee learn that things don't happen by coincidence. Generational forces are at work, keeping promises, protecting family members, and perhaps even drawing Adrian back to the church. For Brecee and Adrian, God has been hard at work, playing matchmaker all along the way for their paths cross at the right time and the right place.

LEAN ON ME, Book 1. No one should have to go it alone... Caregivers sometimes need a little TLC too.

Tabitha Knicely believes in putting family before everything. She may be overwhelmed caring for her beloved great-aunt, but she would never turn her back on the woman who raised her, even if Aunt Tweet's dementia is getting worse. Tabitha is sure she can do this on her own. But when Aunt Tweet ends up on her neighbor's front porch, and the man has the audacity to accuse Tabitha of elder abuse, things go from bad to awful. Marcus Whittington feels a mountain of regret at causing problems for Tabitha and her great-aunt. How was he to know the frail older woman's niece was doing her best? As Marcus gets to know Aunt Tweet and sees how hard Tabitha is fighting to keep everything together, he can't walk away from the pair. Particularly when helping Tabitha care for her great-aunt leads them on a spiritual journey of faith and surrender.

Here For You, Book 2. Rachel Knicely's life has been on hold for six months while she takes care of her great aunt, who has Alzheimer's. Putting her aunt first was an easy decision—accepting that Aunt Tweet is nearing the end of her battle is far more difficult. Nicholas Adams's ministry is comforting those who are sick and homebound. He responds to a request for help for an ailing woman, but when he meets the Knicelys, he realizes Rachel needs the most support. Nicholas is charmed by and attracted to Rachel, but then devastating news brings both a crisis of faith and roadblocks to their budding relationship that neither could have anticipated. This beautifully emotional and clean story contains a hero and heroine who are better at caring for other people than themselves, a dark moment that shakes their faith, and a well-earned happily ever after.

Stand by Me, Book 3. An uplifting story about embracing love and giving others—and yourself—one more chance. When it comes to being a caregiver, Kym Knicely has been there and done that. Then she meets Charles "Chaz" Banks and soon learns that every caregiving situation is different. Chaz takes care of his seven-year-old autistic granddaughter, Chauncy. Although Kym's attraction to Chaz is strong, she has to decide whether a romantic relationship can survive and thrive between two people at different stages in life. It's a journey with a different set of rules that Kym has to play by if she and Chaz are to have their happily ever after and the faith and family they envision.

ABOUT *Waiting for Christmas,*

A chance meeting. An undeniable attraction.

And a first date that starts with a stakeout that leads to a winner-takes-all shopping spree. It's the making of a holiday romance. While philanthropist Sterling Price believes in charitable causes, he and licensed social worker Ciara Summers have a difference of opinion on how to bless others. Ciara is a rebel with a cause and a hundred reasons why helping those less fortunate is important. Sterling is a man of means who believes a financial responsibility comes with giving.

The Lord will make sure everyone's needs are met, and He has something extra for Sterling and Ciara that can't wait until Christmas.

About *Christmas Dinner,*

How do you celebrate the holidays after losing a loved one? Take the journey, beginning with Christmas Dinner. For months, Darcelle Price has suffered depression in silence. But things are about to change as she plans to celebrate Christmas Eve with family and share her journey. Darcelle invites them via group text, not knowing she had included her ex. Evanston Giles is surprised to hear from the woman he loved after months following their breakup. Seeking closure, he shows up on her doorstep for answers. A lot can happen on Christmas Eve. Restoring family ties, building her faith in God, and falling in love again is just the beginning of the night of miracles.

About *Taye's Gift*,

Welcome to Snowflake, Colorado—a small town where wishes come true! When six old high school friends receive a letter that their fellow friend, Charity Hart, wrote before she passed away, their lives take an unexpected turn. She leaves them each a check for $1,500 and asks them to grant a wish—a secret wish—for someone else by Christmas. Who lays off someone before the holidays? Taye Thomas' employer did, so instead of Christmas shopping, she's job hunting. More devastating news comes when an old high school friend passes away. Could God be answering her prayers for help when she learns that Charity Hart left a $1500 check? No, the caveat is it's more blessed to give than receive. Taye has 30 days to find someone else in need to bless. To complicate matters, she's lives in Kansas City, which is more than eight hours away from Snowflake and she can't do it alone. Keeping a secret has never been so much work.

About *Couple by Christmas*,

Holidays haven't been the same for Derek Washington since his divorce. He and his ex-wife, Robyn, go out of their way to avoid each other. This Christmas may be different when he decides to give his son, Tyler, the family he once had before they split. Derek's going to need the Lord's intervention to soften her heart to agree to some outings. God's help doesn't come in the way he expected, but it's all good because everything falls in place for them to be a couple by Christmas.

About *Prayers Answered By Christmas,*

Christmas is coming. While other children are compiling their lists for a fictional Santa, eight-year-old Mikaela Washington is kneeling, making her requests known to the Lord: One mommy for Christmas, please. Portia Hunter refuses to let her ex-husband cheat her out of the family she wants. Her prayer is for God to send the right man into her life. Marlon Washington will do anything for his two little girls, but can he find a mommy for them and a love for himself? Since Christmas is the time of year to remember the many gifts God has given men, maybe these three souls will get their heart s desire.

About *A Noelle for Nathan,*

A Noelle for Nathan is a story of kindness, selflessness, and falling in love during the Christmas season. Andersen Investors & Consultants, LLC, CFO Nathan Andersen (A Christian Christmas) isn't looking for attention when he buys a homeless man a meal, but grade school teacher Noelle Foster is watching his every move with admiration. His generosity makes him a man after her own heart. While donors give more to children and families in need around the holiday season, Noelle Foster believes in giving year-round after seeing many of her students struggle with hunger and finding a warm bed at night. At a second-chance meeting, sparks fly when Noelle and Nathan share a kindred spirit with their passion to help those less fortunate. Whether they're doing charity work or attending Christmas parties, the couple becomes inseparable. Although Noelle and

Nathan exchange gifts, the biggest present is the one from Christ.

One reader says, "A Noelle for Nathan makes you fall in love with love...the love of mankind and the love of God. You cannot read this without wanting to give and do more, all while being appreciative of what you have."

About *Christmas Greetings*,

Saige Carter loves everything about Christmas: the shopping, the food, the lights, and of course, Christmas wouldn't be complete without family and friends to share in the traditions they've created together. Plus, Saige is extra excited about her line of Christmas greeting cards hitting store shelves, but when she gets devastating news around the holidays, she wonders if she'll ever look at Christmas the same again. Daniel Washington is no Scrooge, but he'd rather skip the holidays altogether than spend them with his estranged family. After one too many arguments around the dinner table one year, Daniel had enough and walked away from the drama. As one year has turned into many, no one seems willing to take the first step toward reconciliation. When Daniel reads one of Saige's greeting cards, he's unsure if the words inside are enough to erase the pain and bring about forgiveness. Once God reveals His purpose for their lives to them, they will have a reason to rejoice. *Come unto me, all ye that labor and are heavily laden, and I will give you rest. Take my yoke upon you, and learn of me; for I am meek and lowly in heart: and ye shall find rest unto your souls.* Matthew 11:28-29

About *A Baby for Christmas*,

Yes, diamonds are a girl's best friend, but unless the jewel is going on Solae Wyatt-Palmer's ring finger, they hold little value to her. When she meets Fire Captain Hershel Kavanaugh, their magnetism is undeniable and there's no doubt that it's love at first sight. Since Solae adores Hershel's two boys from his failed marriage, she wouldn't blink at the chance to become a mother to them. But when it seems as if Hershel doesn't have a proposal on his agenda, she has no choice but to cut her losses and move on. But Christmas is coming. And in order to win Solae back, Hershel must resolve some past issues before convincing her that she possesses everything he wants.

About *A Christian Christmas,*

Christmas will never be the same for Joy Knight if Christian Andersen has his way. Not to be confused with a secret Santa, Christian and his family are busier than Santa's elves making sure the Lord's blessings are distributed to those less fortunate by Christmas day. Joy is playing the hand that life dealt her, rearing four children in a home that is on the brink of foreclosure. She's not looking for a handout, but when Christian rescues her in the checkout line; her niece thinks Christian is an angel. Joy thinks he's just another man who will eventually leave, disappointing her and the children. Although Christian is a servant of the Lord, he is a flesh and blood man and all he wants for Christmas is Joy Knight. Can time spent with Christian turn Joy's attention from her financial woes to the real meaning of Christmas—and true love? A Christian Christmas is a holiday novella to be enjoyed at any time of the year.

In *Every Day is Christmas,*

A Christmas ornament, an ailing grandmother, and a match-making sister are all ingredients for a holiday romance.

Landon Michaels is on a mission to fulfill this grandmother's request for a one-of-a-kind Black angel ornament. With dementia setting in, this might be the last Christmas she remembers.

Gina Christmas is the gatekeeper of unique handcrafted ornaments. It's tax season, and the accountant is too busy crunching numbers to track down an ornament, especially since the holiday is months away.

When Granny Lonna wants something, Landon, her favorite and only grandson, is determined to make it happen. But what she wants for Christmas is for Landon to find the perfect love.

PAT SIMMONS INTRODUCES a new Christian fiction series that reminds readers that the bad guys don't always win, especially when the Lord fights our battles.

In *Day Not Promised*, Omega Addams thought it was a typical workday until a detour on the way home changes everything. She's almost killed, but an innocent bystander, Mitchell Franklin, takes a bullet for Omega during a gas station robbery. In the aftermath, Omega has no idea that God expects her to "pray it forward" until a spiritual battle unfolds before her eyes. Another innocent bystander is in trouble; unless Omega gets her prayer life together, others will die without Christ. It's a chain reaction that highlights the responsibility of a Christian—hot, cold, or lukewarm. It's time to get our acts together. We are our brother's keeper.

In *Day She Prayed*, New Christian convert Tally Gilbert knows the power of prayer and the pain of walking away. She's witnessed family and friends' healing, salvation, and deliverance. There's one holdout, and he's at the top of her prayer list. The love of her life, Randall Addams, won't surrender to the Lord, so Tally ends the relationship. What will it take for Randall to turn to God? Will Tally's prayers be answered, or will Randall—and their love—be lost forever?

Don't underestimate a woman who knows how to pray, has backup, and believes "The Word of God is quick, and powerful, and sharper than any two-edged sword, piercing even to the dividing the soul from the spirit, and of the joints and marrow, and is a discerner of the thoughts and intents of the heart." Hebrews 4:12.

If the devil wants a battle, he picks the wrong woman to fight.

In *Days Are Coming*, I'm coming for the children.

Minister Jude Morgan has a strong relationship with the Lord but doesn't know what the latest message means. He is determined to intercede for his young mentee, Carlton Oliver, and children worldwide.

Nine-year-old Carlton wants to get to know his estranged dad, but at what cost? He's about to discover many things he doesn't know about the man who fathered him, and he's on a mission to worship the Lord.

Sinclaire Oliver regrets getting her ex, Harrison Wakefield, involved in her life and that of his son Carlton. He's more trouble than the monthly child support payments she had to sue for. She knows he's angry but never expects it to take a dark turn. Sinclaire learns that God makes no mistakes, even when things don't make sense.

As God sends His judgment on the earth, the devil plants decoys to distract the saints from their mission to be on guard. Is the world doomed, or is there room for redemption?

In *Day of Salvation*, Mother Kincaid, from Christ Is For All Church, has been fervently praying, along with other prayer warriors around the world, for Jesus to return and rescue His saints from this wicked world.

One day, God answers her with a list of unknown individuals who need salvation and a commission for the intercessors and prayer warriors to find and draw them to Christ. Then He will come to redeem His saints, and judgment will begin on the earth.

The caveat to the Lord God's edict: the timer has been set, and if the intercessors don't witness to them, those people will be lost forever.

God thunders, "Get set, get ready, GO!!!!!"